"We had no business kissing like that!"

Tyler caught Julie by the shoulders. "Why not? We're both legal and free."

"All the more reason for us to be careful." She shook off his touch and walked to the end of the deck, to the exact spot where they had first kissed eight years ago.

Tyler followed. "All I'm asking is what's so bad about our being together?"

"I'll tell you what's so bad," Julie answered, suddenly furious with herself. "How you make me feel, that's what. It isn't right. It isn't good. It isn't even—"

Tyler's lips smothered the rest of her sentence, which was forgotten in the wake of one devastating kiss. Clearly she had no willpower where he was concerned.

Clearly, he knew it....

Linda Varner brings you the joy of the holiday season with three very special couples who discover a HOME FOR THE HOLIDAYS...and forever.

WON'T YOU BE MY HUSBAND? (11/96)
MISTLETOE BRIDE (12/96)
NEW YEAR'S WIFE (1/97)

Dear Reader,

This month Silhouette Romance has six irresistible novels for you, starting with our FABULOUS FATHERS selection, *Mad for the Dad* by Terry Essig. When a sexy single man becomes an instant dad to a toddler, the independent divorcée next door offers parenthood lessons—only to dream of marriage and motherhood all over again!

In *Having Gabriel's Baby* by Kristin Morgan, our BUNDLES OF JOY book, a fleeting night of passion with a handsome, brooding rancher leaves Joelle in the family way—and the dad-to-be insisting on a marriage of convenience for the sake of the baby....

Years ago Julie had been too young for the dashing man of her dreams. Now he's back in town, and Julie's still hoping he'll make her his bride in *New Year's Wife* by Linda Varner, part of her miniseries HOME FOR THE HOLIDAYS.

What's a man to do when he has no interest in marriage but is having trouble resisting the lovely, warm and wonderful woman in his life? Get those cold feet to the nearest wedding chapel in *Family Addition* by Rebecca Daniels.

In *About That Kiss* by Jayne Addison, Joy Mackey, sister of the bride, is sure her sis's ex-fiancé has returned to sabotage the wedding. But his intention is to walk down the aisle with Joy!

And finally, when a woman shows up on a bachelor doctor's doorstep with a baby that looks just like him, everyone in town mistakenly thinks the tiny tot is his in Christine Scott's *Groom on the Loose*.

Enjoy!

Melissa Senate, Senior Editor

NEW YEAR'S WIFE

Linda Varner

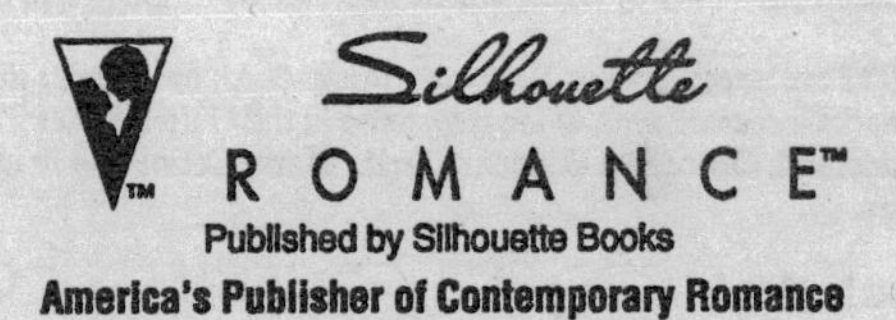

Published by Silhouette Books
America's Publisher of Contemporary Romance

Special thanks to pilots Jack and Sharon Davis for their suggestions, advice and critique.

ISBN 0-373-19200-2

NEW YEAR'S WIFE

This edition published by arrangement with Harlequin Books S.A.

Printed in U.S.A.

Books by Linda Varner

Silhouette Romance

Heart of the Matter #625
Heart Rustler #644
The Luck of the Irish #665
Honeymoon Hideaway #698
Better To Have Loved #734
A House Becomes a Home #780
Mistletoe and Miracles #835
As Sweet as Candy #851
Diamonds Are Forever #868
A Good Catch #906
Something Borrowed #943
Firelight and Forever #966
**Dad on the Job* #1036
**Believing in Miracles* #1051
**Wife Most Unlikely* #1068
†Won't You Be My Husband? #1088
†Mistletoe Bride #1193
†New Year's Wife #1200

*Mr. Right, Inc.
†Home for the Holidays

LINDA VARNER

confesses she is a hopeless romantic. Nothing is more thrilling, she believes, than the battle of wits between a man and a woman who are meant for each other but just don't know it yet! Linda enjoys writing romance and considers herself very lucky to have been both a RITA finalist and a third-place winner in the National Readers' Choice Awards in 1993.

A full-time federal employee, Linda lives in Arkansas with her husband and their two children. She loves to hear from readers. Write to her at 813 Oak St., Suite 10A-277, Conway, AR 72032.

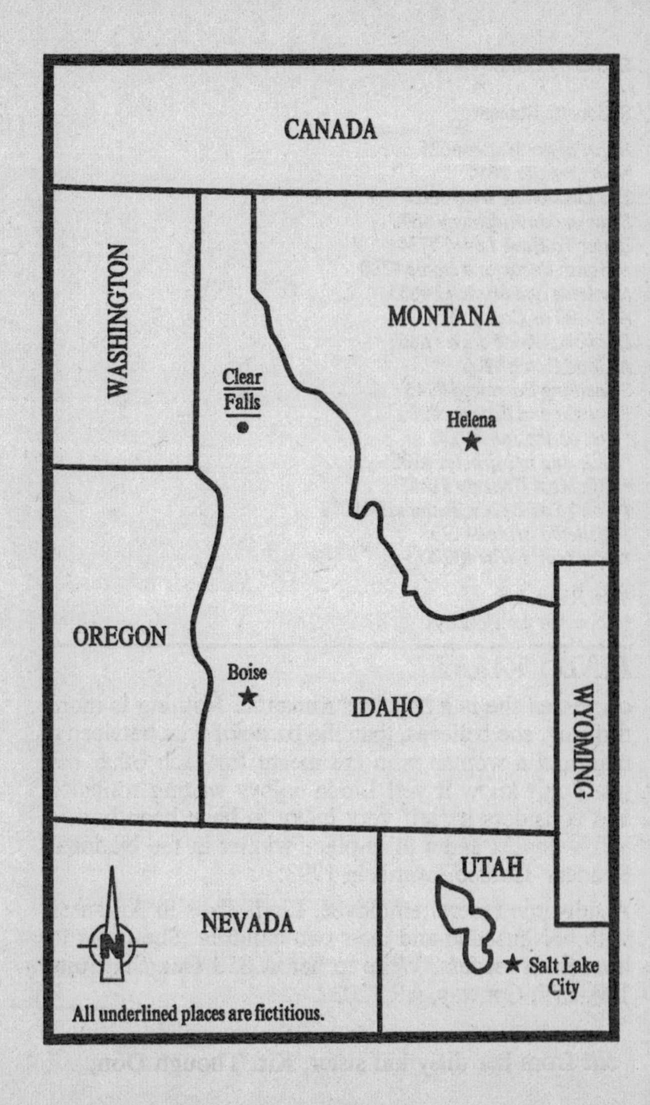
CANADA
WASHINGTON
MONTANA
Clear Falls
Helena
OREGON
Boise
IDAHO
WYOMING
UTAH
NEVADA
N
Salt Lake City
All underlined places are fictitious.

Prologue

"Yo, Ty! Would you see if the birthday gal's out on the back porch? It's twenty minutes till a brand new year—*party time!*—and we can't find her anywhere."

Tyler Jordan nodded agreement to Don Newman, host of this fun and confusion. Winding his way through the jam-packed room, bright with streamers and bobbing balloons, Tyler dodged more than one guest wearing a colorful party hat and wielding the noisy blow-outs provided earlier. He chuckled as he slipped into the kitchen, then headed straight out the back door to look for Julie, one of Don's two younger sisters.

Tyler saw her at once, standing alone and bathed in moonlight at the far end of the porch that stretched across the rear of the rambling Victorian house. Instead of calling out, he just stared for a moment at the slender brunette, marveling that she could be so different from her ditsy kid sister, Kit. Though Don, a college classmate, seldom talked about his female siblings, he had once commented that the oldest was "legal." Tyler, of course, had figured out which was which the moment he met the two girls upon his arrival earlier that evening.

He now crept forward, not stopping until he stood just behind his favorite of Don's sisters. "So you're not a missing person after all, but a star gazer."

"Yes," she murmured, as though somehow she'd known he was there all the time. "Aren't they gorgeous tonight?"

"Breathtaking," Tyler answered. He ignored the night sky, instead gluing his gaze to the dark-eyed beauty who'd stolen his heart. Julie laughed, obviously pleased by the offhanded compliment.

"It's almost midnight," she said after a moment's silence.

"Which is why Don sent me out here to get you."

Julie nodded that she'd guessed that. Turning her back to the yard, she leaned against the ornate iron rail that edged the porch, then crossed her arms over her chest in a self-hug Tyler wished he could help her with. Her bold gaze swept Tyler from head to toe.

"So what do you think of our midnight birthday party tradition?"

"I think it's perfect for someone born at 12:01 on January first." Tyler, too, leaned against the rail, so close that the smell of her cologne instantly assailed him. The subtle floral scent brought to mind sunrise streaming through an open window, crisp cotton sheets and lazy wake-up kisses that led to morning love.

At once Tyler wished he could whisk Julie away to just such a place. They'd celebrate her birthday with a private party neither would forget. That is, if he hadn't imagined the incredible instantaneous chemistry between them when they were first introduced. Had he? Tyler had to wonder, risking a sidelong glance in Julie's direction. At that moment she shivered violently, and he realized why she hugged herself.

"My God!" he exclaimed. "You don't even have on a coat."

"You could share yours," she suggested.

Tyler hastily unzipped the leather bomber jacket that was a gift from his parents on his twenty-second birthday, four years ago. He opened the front of it wide in invitation. Julie stepped up to let him share his warmth. Conveniently, Tyler's temperature shot up another couple of degrees, and his heart began to thump erratically against his rib cage.

Wired as he was, Tyler didn't trust himself to do anything more than hold the jacket around her with a loose hug, his chin resting on the top of her head. To his delight, Julie slipped her arms around his waist and pressed her body closer.

Green light? he wondered, even as she tipped her head back and met his questioning gaze square on. She smiled at him, a sexy smile that was an unmistakable invitation.

Accepting it but still holding back, Tyler did nothing more than touch his lips to hers in a brief, brushing kiss. Julie sighed with what could only be frustration. Reaching up to clasp her hands behind his neck, she took the initiative, tugging his head down to press her mouth fully to his. Her tongue teased for entry, sending a shock wave clear to Tyler's toes. Groaning his defeat, Tyler gave in to their mutual desire, parting his lips, then taking control of the kiss.

And what a kiss it was! Wet, wild and wonderful...but not enough to satisfy him. Not nearly enough.

How could it be when Julie seemed to be everything he'd ever dreamed of? Her heated response set him on fire, and at once hungry for whatever he could coax from her, Tyler planted kisses on Julie's cheeks, nose, chin and neck. Ah, but she tasted good...so damn good.

Tyler felt Julie slip her hands under his sweater. Lightly she raked her fingernails over his bare back, an incredibly tantalizing action that further fueled his need. Tyler responded by palming each of her breasts in turn through the thick yarn of her oversize sweater.

But even that wasn't enough—not when she was so willing, so obviously excited by his touch. Taking his cue from Julie, Tyler slipped his hands under her sweater and traced with his fingertips the lace-encased fullness hidden there. Her breasts seemed to swell to his touch. The tips grew noticeably taut. Her breaths became soft pants that Tyler's kiss stole away. His body tensed, strategic parts hard and ready for love.

He struggled with the front clasp of her bra. Somewhere nearby a door slammed.

Tyler leapt back, his own breath now ragged. A quick glance round revealed that they were still alone. Gulping audibly, Tyler looked down at Julie, now a good three feet away and obviously rattled. They exchanged a rueful glance, then shared a guilty laugh.

"Something's happening here," he blurted, anxious to let her know how serious he was about this.

Julie's smile instantly vanished. She nodded solemnly, but said nothing.

"I didn't expect this." He could barely get the words out, suddenly and uncharacteristically flustered, thanks to this woman he'd met mere hours ago. "I just came to Idaho to ski."

She nodded again.

"Don told me he had two sisters, but I never dreamed—" Tyler swallowed hard again. "I never dreamed one of them—" He shook his head, completely at a loss for words. "God, but you're beautiful."

Her smile lit up the night.

Tyler relaxed and smiled back. "We'll just take this thing slow, okay?"

"Slow?" Her twinkling eyes challenged him.

Tyler chuckled. "Well, maybe not."

For a moment they just looked at each other, then Tyler cleared his throat rather loudly. "I, um, guess you'd better go in. Don's going to send out a search party if you don't."

"You're not coming?" Julie caught hold of his arm as if she feared he'd suddenly vanish into the night.

"In a minute." He did not add that he needed time alone to cool down. Surely she knew. They'd been standing so close....

"Promise?" Suddenly she sounded more like her teenaged sister than the mature young woman that she was.

Tyler, charmed by her unexpected air of innocence, nodded. "Nothing could keep me away, Julie. *Nothing.*"

With obvious reluctance, she left him and entered the house. Moments later, Tyler heard her guests cheer a welcome. Anxious to join the midnight fun, he sucked in a lungful of frosty air and willed his love-tense body to relax. He thought of the week that lay ahead and vowed to spend every hour with Julie, a woman like no other, surely the woman of his dreams. Several minutes of fantasizing about the days to come slipped by before Tyler came to with a start and glanced at his watch. Cursing softly, he spun and headed straight for the kitchen.

Just as he stepped through the door a noisy countdown to the New Year's birthday began in the next room.

"Ten . . . nine . . . eight . . ."

Determined not to miss a millisecond of Julie's special night Tyler quickened his pace.

"Seven . . . six . . ."

Just before he got to the living room door, he spied a two-tiered, heart-shaped birthday cake sitting on the table. It had not been there earlier.

"Five . . . four . . ."

The fancy red writing on it leapt out at him.

"Three . . . two.."

Tyler stumbled to a halt.

"One!"

And read the words.

Wild cheers and congratulations echoed off the walls, but Tyler stood in stunned silence, staring at the sentiment that changed his life forever and not for good.

Happy Birthday, Julie.

17.

Chapter One

Eight years later

"Happy birthday, Sis."

"Thanks," Julie Newman McCrae replied, setting down a warm pitcher of spiced apple cider so she could accept the hug that Kit Porter, her older sister by four years, offered to her.

"So tell me, how does it feel to be twenty-five?" Kit might as well have been asking how it felt to be a leper. She looked that horrified.

Julie shrugged. "So far it's not a bit different than twenty-four... or twenty-three... for that matter."

"Oh, but it is," Kit teased, brown eyes twinkling. "And I'll tell you why." She glanced around as if to make sure no one eavesdropped, then leaned close, whispering, "The big three-oh is just *five years away now.*"

"Only *one* for you," Julie retorted.

The redhead groaned and sagged against her sister. "Oh God, don't remind me."

Laughing, they shared a sympathetic hug.

"Donnie boy is finally here." Kit ran a hand through her short, copper-colored hair, a genetic throwback from an Irish great-great. "And he's brought someone with him."

"So what else is new?" Julie questioned. One of her older brothers worked public relations for New-Ware, their father's cookware business, and had more friends than an Idaho winter had snowflakes. He was forever bringing one or another of them to Clear Falls, where the six-bedroom, three-story home owned by Julie's dad, widower John Newman, was located. Luckily she had planned her birthday party refreshments with that in mind. "I have plenty to eat tonight."

"Yeah, well they both have suitcases," Kit advised. "Not to mention skis. So you may have more than tonight to worry about."

Julie sighed at that news, though she didn't really mind it. Of all the household tasks she'd taken on in exchange for rent-free accommodations, cooking was the one she liked most and did best. She got plenty of practice, too. In the five months since her dad had suggested the trade-off and she'd agreed to it, they'd been alone together in the house for maybe a week.

Julie's dad blamed that on their proximity to the ski slopes. Julie blamed it on his big heart. After all, who had talked her oldest brother, Sid, into leaving his two stepchildren and his baby in Idaho while he and his wife explored European markets for New-Ware? Who had demanded Kit move back home, when her sailor husband was stationed on an aircraft carrier? And who always insisted that Don stay at the house whenever he was in town, whether or not he had girlfriends, co-workers or buddies in tow?

John Newman, that's who.

"Well, I hope they have an appetite for cold cuts, dips and leftover birthday cake," Julie murmured, picking up the pitcher again and slipping out the door of the kitchen so she could hug that rascal of a brother she hadn't seen for a month. "Because that's what we're going to have for days to come."

A second later she deposited the pitcher on the buffet table. Ever the perfect hostess—at home and at the New-Ware cooking demonstrations that were her source of income—Julie assessed the table to see if it lacked anything else.

It didn't, and gratefully she wound her way through the crush of friends and relatives to where her brother and his companion stood talking.

Don, a handsome young man by even a stranger's standards, looked especially wonderful to his little sister tonight. Though six years separated their ages, Julie had always been particularly close to him.

"Don!" she exclaimed when still several feet away. He turned, all smiles, and engulfed her in a bear hug that threatened her rib cage. "You just missed the countdown."

"Sorry about that," he said with a shrug of apology, adding, "Happy New Year."

"Same to you," she replied.

"And happy birthday." Don set her back on her feet. "How does it feel to be twenty-five?"

Julie smiled at his unwitting echo of Kit's earlier question. "You should know. You were there *six* years ago."

"Low blow," Don scolded, but he laughed. "I brought someone with me," he said. "I ran into him at the gas station on the corner, and since he didn't have motel reservations anywhere, I talked him into staying here a night or two. Dad seemed pleased. I hope you don't mind."

"Hey, I'm just a guest, myself," Julie replied with a laugh, for the first time shifting her full attention to Don's companion.

"Hi, I'm Julie McCrae," she said, automatically extending her hand to him as she raised her gaze to meet his—dark, intense and too, too familiar. At once Julie was hurled back in time eight years to a birthday party just like this one.

She forgot her name. She forgot her manners. She forgot how to breathe—astonishing reactions that floored her.

"Actually, I think you two have already met," Don commented, apparently oblivious to her life-threatening discomfiture. "This is—"

"*Tyrone,* right?" she blurted, desperate that this man now holding her hand so tightly would never guess what he'd done to her fragile, teenaged ego at that party so long ago.

"Tyler," he solemnly corrected. "Tyler Jordan."

"Oops," Julie said, adding a who-cares-anyway laugh. She tugged her fingers free of his and swiped them down her black wool pants. "Sorry. I'm terrible with names, but I never forget a face. How long has it been since we last, um, *spoke?* Six years, seven?"

"Eight years, eleven minutes and—" he glanced at his watch "—thirty seconds. At a party just like this one."

Julie nearly choked and glanced quickly at Don. She'd never told anyone about the intimacies shared with Tyler just before midnight so long ago out on the porch.

Did this mean Tyler had?

But Don just laughed and slapped his old friend on the back—an act of affection that meant he didn't know the truth. Julie, of course, should've guessed that. Don had bored her with more than one tale of Tyler's dangerous—no, foolhardy—exploits through the years, things Don would never have told her if he'd been aware of what had happened between them. "No wonder you didn't argue when I invited you to come home with me. You remember what great parties my little sis throws."

"Yeah," Tyler agreed with a half smile. "What *great parties* she throws." His gaze dropped to Julie's mouth and lingered there. Immediately she wondered if it were her parties he remembered or her kisses. But no, it couldn't be her kisses. He'd long since proved that they—and everything else about her—were totally forgettable.

Unfortunately such wasn't the case for Julie, who suddenly remembered not only the kisses they'd shared but the caresses that had accompanied them. And then there had been that awful moment later when she'd been forced to face the fact that Tyler had only been playing with her out on the porch....

A little surprised by the vividness of her memories, Julie gave herself a get-it-together shake. Surely she wasn't still mourning a relationship that had never existed anywhere except in her fanciful, teenage head.

"And speaking of birthdays," Don continued, bringing her back to the here and now, "I've brought you a present from Uncle Sy.'' He looked at Tyler and winked. ''It's special. Really special.''

Julie looked at her brother's empty hands, then all around. ''Where is it?''

''In the garage.'' Don grinned.

''The garage?'' She turned toward the back of the house, fully intending to step out the kitchen door and see whatever her eccentric uncle, Silas Newman, had sent. Don stopped her with an outflung arm.

''Not yet. I want Dad to get the camera, and I want all your guests to come watch.''

Though avidly curious now, Julie obeyed. She eyed Don rather suspiciously as he ushered their dad, Kit and the guests in the direction of the garage, knowing he wasn't above playing a good practical joke on her. And while she usually didn't mind them, she wasn't at all sure she could handle another surprise this night.

On that thought, Julie shifted her gaze to her first surprise, still standing next to her, his gaze on Don. Discreetly she assessed him—the man who'd broken her teenage heart so long ago. He looked older than his age, which she'd always assumed to be the same as Don's. In fact, she could have sworn she saw a silver strand or two gleaming in his otherwise brown hair. And there were wrinkles around his eyes, too—little crow's feet that the sun had most likely furrowed into his skin.

Or had hard living engraved them there? After all, it must be tough to seduce a woman at every port, or in his case, on every mountain.

Woman? Julie almost laughed. Not by a long shot. Just a teen with raging hormones, too easily flattered by big brother's dashing college friend. She should have known that Tyler hadn't meant a word he said.

And she should've gotten over it long ago.

At that moment, Tyler's gaze found and locked with Julie's. She jumped as if he'd reached out and touched her. Then, acutely embarrassed, she brushed past him to hurry up Don. Julie managed one step away before Tyler caught her by the arm.

"I'd really like to speak with you," he said. "To explain... and apologize."

"Whatever for?" Julie responded, easing her arm free. God, but he was still gorgeous. And at Tyler's touch, every hormone in her body—hormones surely older and wiser—sprang to life and waved for attention just the way they had the first time she met him. Rattled, sweating, Julie could barely fake a smile.

Tyler laughed—a humorless sound. "I know damn good and well you remember what happened at your birthday party eight years ago. In fact...if I didn't know better, I'd say you're still pretty steamed." He sounded as if he couldn't believe it, either.

"About something that happened that long ago? Trust me, Tyler, I've had much better things to do than carry a grudge against you. Besides, if anyone should apologize, it's me for trailing after you like some little lost pup that first evening we met. As for that midnight fooling around—"

"Stop it!" Tyler hissed, stepping so close she had to tip her head back to meet his gaze.

But meet it she did. "You don't owe me an explanation or an apology. That's water way under the bridge. Now please excuse me. I have guests and a party to attend to."

"Fine," he coolly replied. "We'll talk later. When everyone is gone."

"Everyone will never be gone," she said, stepping back to put precious inches between them. "In case you hadn't noticed, this house is a lot like Grand Central Station...or maybe the Grand *Hotel* would be more appropriate?''

He winced, clearly picking up on the jibe. ''I won't hang around here long. Hell, I won't hang around at all—if you'll talk with me tonight.''

''Stay as long as you like,'' she said. ''It's nothing to me.'' With that, Julie whirled and hurried to Don and her dad, who had his video camera in hand.

At the sight of her grinning parent, Julie instantly regretted her rudeness to Tyler. Her father had seemed so lost since the death of Julie's mother almost nine months ago. Knowing how devastating it was to lose a spouse, she suspected that loneliness was the main reason he'd begged her to come live with him again and not any desire to help her save rent money.

''Are you ready?'' Don asked. His bright eyes and flushed cheeks bespoke his excitement, and Julie made a special effort to push her disturbing encounter with Tyler out of her head.

''Past ready,'' she replied, trying to muster enthusiasm for Uncle Sy's gift.

''Good. Now stay put until everyone is set, okay?''

''Okay,'' Julie promised, biting back a smile. She felt a stirring of excitement. Never had she seen Don so worked up. What on earth awaited her out in the garage?

''Come on, Dad.'' Don led the way to the back door, through which Tyler had just vanished. His dad grinned mysteriously at Julie, then followed. Don did the same.

Julie, blessedly alone for the moment, sucked in a couple of deep breaths to compose herself before she trailed her brother out the door. At first she saw nothing but her guests, standing all in a bunch. Then they stepped aside, en masse, to reveal . . . a car.

And not just any car—a wickedly red 1956 Corvette convertible in mint condition.

Julie *knew* this because she'd pointed out this very machine countless times at Uncle Sy's Seattle automobile museum where she had worked so many summers. It was the most popular exhibit there.

Was.

Now, for some reason, it sat in her dad's garage.

"Voilà!" Don exclaimed, flinging out his hand, palm upward, in the direction of the Corvette.

The car? Uncle Sy wanted her to have the car? Julie caught her breath. "You can't mean . . . ?"

"I do."

"Oh my God." At once Julie's knees threatened to buckle. She clutched Kit's arm for support, took several fortifying breaths, then moved, trancelike, toward the sleek roadster. Slowly she walked around it, touching first a fender, next a headlight and last the windshield.

"Well?" Don prompted when she'd completed her inspection.

"It's real," Julie announced. Her guests exploded into laughter . . . and congratulations.

"Get in," John Newman prompted over the din, his eye to the camera.

Julie nodded rather numbly and obeyed. Once behind the wheel, she touched the dash, the radio, the white leather seat next to her . . . fully expecting everything to vanish. When they didn't, she grasped the wheel, tossed her head back and closed her eyes, already imagining herself speeding down some scenic highway—mountains all around, blue sky and sunshine overhead, hair blowing in the wind.

"What a car. *What a car.*" It was Kit, now sitting in the passenger seat. Julie looked at her in surprise—she hadn't even heard the other door open. "Do you know what this baby's worth?"

"Yes," Julie said. At once she felt guilty. Though Uncle Sy had always been generous with his many nephews and nieces, he'd never given any of them something so expensive.

"Now don't you worry about it," Kit whispered as though reading her mind. "Apparently all the Newman cousins will get one when Uncle Sy dies. He just wanted you to have yours now. Dad's supposed to send him the videotape so he can see your reaction."

"But what did I ever do to deserve a gift like this?" Julie asked.

"You lived and worked with that old man for—" Kit frowned "—how many summers?"

"Six."

"Well that's six more than anyone else could've. Believe me, honey, you earned this car."

Suddenly car keys dangled before Julie's eyes. "Why don't you take her for a spin?" Don suggested. "The roads are dry."

"But my guests..."

"Dad's taking care of them."

Julie looked up to find that only three people remained in the garage besides herself—Don, Kit and...Tyler.

Tyler. She'd almost forgotten him in the excitement. But there he stood, not three feet away, as classically American as her little red sports car and every bit as dashing...damn him. His eyes never left her, and not sure how much more her poor old heart could take this night, Julie snatched the keys from Don.

"Yes!" Kit fairly bounced with excitement in the seat.

Don stepped away from the car. Julie inserted the key into the ignition. She paused before starting the engine, taking a moment to familiarize herself with the car. She saw the gear selector, the accelerator, the brake pedal and the...clutch. At once her soaring spirits took a nosedive.

"Oh, no."

"What's wrong?" Don demanded, instantly by her side again.

"It has a standard transmission," Julie moaned.

"But of course it does...." His jaw dropped. "You mean you *still* can't drive a standard?"

"No."

"You're kidding!" Kit exclaimed.

Julie glared at her. "You mean *you* can?"

"Yes, as a matter of fact." Kit looked very smug. "Monty taught me." Monty was Kit's absent husband.

"Then you can teach me."

"Okay...but not this week. I'm working split shifts at Clearwater Regional so I'll be out more than in."

Julie just shook her head. How Kit, who worked as a relief nurse all over town, ever kept her complicated schedule straight Julie just didn't know.

"I can teach you," Don said.

"When?" Julie demanded.

"Whenever you want," he replied. Then he frowned. "Except... It's officially Saturday, isn't it? I've got top salesmen arriving around nine a.m. I have to pick them up and get them settled at their hotels. Actually, I guess

I'll pretty much have to entertain them during the day until next Sunday."

"You mean neither of you can help me before next weekend?" Julie heaved a heartfelt sigh of disappointment.

"Maybe Dad would show you how," Kit suggested.

"I'm sure he would," Julie replied. "I'm also sure neither of us would survive the experience." She well remembered another driving lesson—back when she was a teenager yearning for a license. Apparently Kit remembered it, too, for she winced.

"Why don't we go inside and ask for a volunteer?" Don asked. "Surely one of our guests would be willing to take you on."

"No!" Julie replied, so loudly that her brother jumped. "If you so much as hint to those people I can't drive this car you are a dead man, understand?"

Eyes twinkling, Don nodded.

"I have some time on my hands," Tyler said. "*I'll* teach you."

Julie's heart somersaulted at the unexpected suggestion. "No thanks—"

"But that's a great idea," Don argued, cutting off her refusal.

"Yeah, great," Kit echoed with enthusiasm. Clearly both of them thought Tyler's idea the perfect solution.

Unfortunately, Julie didn't. Her gaze locked with Tyler's. She noted that a hint of a smile—no doubt of triumph—now turned up the corners of his mouth.

"I couldn't ask you to do that," she murmured, vastly irritated. She opened the car door and stepped out on the pavement.

"You don't have to ask," Tyler replied. "I've already volunteered."

"That's very generous, but I—" Julie broke off, suddenly aware of Don's and Kit's puzzled frowns. They didn't understand her dilemma—never would, unless she told them everything. Julie had no intention of admitting she'd never gotten over that two seconds' worth of foreplay eight years ago.

So why not keep things simple and accept his offer? Julie asked herself. A possible argument sprang to mind immediately: she didn't want to spend a single moment alone with Tyler. Didn't want to hear the explanation or the apology that would justify what he'd done back then and eliminate all excuses not to fall for him again.

Not that she really would....

Although deadly attractive with those chiseled features and that rugged jawline, Tyler Jordan was undoubtedly as much of a daredevil as ever and, therefore, totally incompatible to her current goals of marriage to a rock-solid man and lots of babies. Ignorance of what she really wanted had contributed to her devastation when he left so abruptly all those years ago. Inexperience then exaggerated the impact of the encounter, etching it so indelibly on her brain.

Or perhaps the problem was the nature of their parting. He was unfinished business for sure. As for her physical reaction to him now...a momentary lapse, nothing more.

"Are you sure you don't mind?" Julie therefore asked, adding a sweet smile. "I mean...you did come to the mountains to ski."

"I'll still have time for that." He returned her smile, revealing teeth that flashed gypsy white against his naturally bronze-toned skin.

Julie gulped at the sight and wondered briefly if she hadn't just made the biggest mistake of her life. Then she gave herself a mental kick in the backside. They would only be together an hour, maybe two at the most. She could keep her hands to herself for that long—*would have to* if she intended to shift gears and steer. "All right then. How about later this morning, after we sleep off the party?"

"Fine with me," he replied, cheerfully adding, "And don't you worry. After a week or so of lessons, you'll be a pro. I guarantee it."

Chapter Two

A glass-domed anniversary clock on the mantel chimed the time—3:00 a.m. Tyler Jordan, a volunteer member of the clean-up crew, worked his way through the living room, picking up abandoned paper plates and disposable plastic cups to toss into a trash bag. He battled with his conscience, knowing full well that Julie wanted him to leave, but reluctant to do so until he explained his behavior all those years ago.

So what if she'd already told him she didn't care why he ran away? Her body language said she lied, and even if she spoke the truth, he needed to say his piece. Tyler hated unfinished business. This was definitely that—and the *only* reason he'd abandoned his ski plans so abruptly when he'd run into Don at the gas station.

Don's news that Julie was now widowed had nothing to do with anything. It was the birthday party and the fact that Julie lived with her dad again that cinched the impulsive decision to drop by. When presented with the perfect opportunity to right old wrongs, Tyler had made the most of it. Any man with scruples would, and heaven knew he could claim more than his share of those—the very reason he'd landed himself in this mess.

"I'm on my way out to the trash barrel. Want me to take that for you?" Don reached for the bag Tyler held. "This was the last bag in the box, but I think there are more in the pantry. Go ask Julie."

With a glance around the still-littered room, Tyler nodded and made a beeline to the kitchen, hoping to catch Don's sister alone. If they could talk now, he wouldn't have to sleep over. Contrary to what he'd told her brother, Tyler did have accommodations for tonight—a motel room he'd already put on his credit card and would have to pay for whether or not he utilized it. Fairly certain he wasn't welcome at the Newman house—at least by Julie—Tyler preferred utilizing it.

Worse, he'd paid a hefty entrance fee for a downhill skiing competition on a slope the locals had dubbed GR—Grim Reaper. Tyler planned to win the race and add another trophy to his growing collection.

A push on the swing door later, Tyler stepped into the kitchen, painted bright yellow and trimmed in blue gingham. Julie stood alone with the dishwasher she loaded. Since she didn't look up when he entered, he paused for a moment to study her, just as he'd done eight years ago.

The years had been kind. She was almost the same size as when a teen, though a little more filled out, as mature women usually are. Her brunette hair hung to just below her shoulders, slightly curled on the ends and gleaming reddish in the light. And though she had her back to him, he knew feathery bangs framed her oval face.

For just a second Tyler closed his eyes and pictured that girl-next-door face. He saw wide brown eyes with thick lashes. He saw an uptilted nose and dimples. He saw a friendly smile.

Encouraged by his vision, Tyler stepped closer, something she hadn't allowed all evening. Whistling, busy, Julie didn't seem to notice his soundless approach until he stood mere inches away. Then she stiffened, whirled and stepped back, crimson-glossed lips still pursed for the tune. Tyler's gaze focused first on those full, kissable lips, which had once touched his, then dropped to her breasts, which rose and fell with every agitated breath. He remembered how silky her skin felt to the touch—how incredibly responsive she was. His heart skipped a beat.

"Don't you ever give up?" Julie snapped, self-consciously brushing off her bulky maroon sweater at the exact spot where he'd been staring.

"I didn't come in here to talk," Tyler retorted, a half truth. "I came to get another trash bag."

"Oh." She looked flustered, embarrassed. "I thought...well, it doesn't matter." Pushing up her sleeves, she crossed the room to the walk-in pantry, opened the door and disappeared from view.

Tyler sagged against the counter and struggled to get a grip on his emotions—not an easy thing to do. There was something about this woman—had been from the moment he'd met her—that kept him off balance. She was a magnet to his steel.

She drew his gaze. She annihilated his composure.

She turned him on.

Tyler couldn't explain it and didn't like it, but the fact remained: Julie Newman McCrae had power over him, power she didn't even know she possessed...thank God.

Just thinking about it made Tyler's forehead bead with cold sweat because this time, *this time,* she was legal.

"Julie?" He sort of croaked the word.

At once, she stuck her head out from behind the pantry door and frowned at him. "What?"

"I lied. I did come in here to talk."

She huffed her opinion of that and stepped from the pantry, new box of trash bags in hand. "For crying out loud, Tyler! Can't we just forget about what happened? It's old news. Very old news. And doesn't even matter."

"Then why are you still angry with me?"

"I'm *not.*" They stood toe-to-toe now, separated only by the width of the box she thrust at him.

"The hell you aren't," he retorted. "Your face is red. Your hands are trembling, and for two cents I'll bet you'd throw that box at me."

For a second Julie said nothing, then she heaved a lusty sigh. "To be honest, I'd do it for free, which means I *am* still upset. Unfortunately I can't begin to tell you why, since I didn't even know it until tonight." She shook her head in disbelief. "What happened between us all those years ago is nothing compared to what I've been through since, yet for some reason I'm still irritated about it."

"Then let me explain...please. And we'll put it to rest once and for good."

"Oh, all right," she said after another hesitation. "Explain if you must, but I can't promise I'll like you any better. If I've held a grudge this long, I'll probably take it to the grave." She set the box on the counter and crossed her arms over her chest, clearly waiting for him to speak.

At once Tyler's wits took a leave of absence, taking along his tongue. He felt his face heat, a sure sign he, too, blushed.

"I...uh...well...uh..." *Damn it.* Tyler took a deep breath and tried again. "Do you think we could step out to the porch? Your brother will probably burst in here the moment I—"

As if on cue, Don pushed through the swing door. "What's the holdup?" His gaze leapt from the box of bags to Tyler to Julie. "So are you two going to talk all night or get on with the show? It's 3:00 a.m. I've had several beers too many, and I'd like to get a couple of hours shut-eye before I have to get up again...."

Wordlessly Julie extracted two bags from the box. She gave both men one and then turned her back on them, busy once more with the dishwasher.

Don glanced around the room. "Where are Kit and Dad?"

"Kit has to work tomorrow, er, today, so I sent her to bed an hour ago," Julie told him without glancing up from her work. "As for Dad, since he'll be up again at dawn with Timbo, I waived his KP duties altogether."

"My brother's three-year-old stepson," Don said to Tyler by way of explanation. "He also has a step-daughter named Carly, and a baby of his own, Josh. 'Gramps' volunteered to baby-sit." Don explained the situation as he led the way to the door, which he held open for Tyler. "You do remember that Dad manufactures gourmet pots and pans?"

"I remember." Short of looking as if he didn't want to help out, Tyler had no choice but to step back into the formal living room. Though a bit frustrated at first, he soon decided to make use of Don's presence to fill in a few blanks. "Um...Julie's a widow, right?" he asked as he continued clean up.

"Uh-huh. Her late husband, Cord, was an Alaskan Smoke Jumper—ever heard of them?"

"Sure I have," Tyler murmured, shocked by a stab of what felt suspiciously like jealousy. Alaskan Smoke Jumpers were men's men, noted for their courage and skill. Tyler couldn't begin to compete with one of them.

Compete? With a dead man? At once ashamed of his misguided envy, not to mention his lack of sympathy for Julie, Tyler sharply corralled his emotions. "How long were they married?"

"Just under four years. Though Julie has never said anything, I've always suspected the marriage was not a happy one. They were a mismatch, in my opinion. She's the kind of gal who wants the traditional stone cottage, complete with white picket fence and a yard full of kids. He preferred a log cabin in the woods, big enough for two, but not for three. He also had this thing about physical challenges—" Don chuckled "—something you can relate to, I guess. Why, it was nothing for him to skip Christmas with the family so he could climb a mountain somewhere."

"And Julie moved home right after the funeral?"

"Well, back to Idaho, anyway. That was about a year ago, I guess. She's been working for Dad half of that time and living here in the house since a few months after my mom passed away."

"I heard about your mom. I'm sorry."

Don nodded, and the men worked in silence for a moment.

"Does Kit work for your dad, too?"

"Kit's a nurse," Don said. "She was the wild child—the rebel who didn't want any part of the family business." He shook his head and grinned. "You'd be surprised how many people assume she's the baby of the family."

"Actually... I wouldn't." Tyler cleared his throat, a self-conscious sound to his own ear, though Don didn't react to it. "Kit's married?" At the party he'd noticed that she wore a wide gold band.

Don explained his sister's circumstances, adding, "Her husband, Monty, has another five months on the carrier, then he'll be out for good. I'm assuming they'll find a place of their own, though not if Dad has any say in the matter. He invented the always-room-for-one-more concept, in case you hadn't noticed."

"I had," Tyler admitted.

"You're still with Sky Flight, I guess?" Don asked, referring to the commercial airline for which Tyler had piloted the last five years.

"No. I left them about this time last year."

Don straightened, a look of surprise on his face. "I thought you loved your job there."

Tyler hesitated, not for the first time at a loss for words to verbalize the restlessness that had prompted his leaving the best job he'd ever had. "I needed a change, a challenge."

"So what are you doing now?"

"Nothing until spring. Then I'll probably do what I did last year—charter work, some crop dusting."

"Are you still into stuff like mountain climbing, white-water rafting, motorcycle racing, bungee jumping... ?"

"I didn't do any bungee jumping at all last summer."

"Came to your senses?"

"Nah. I just didn't have time for it. I was too busy with the county fairs."

Don frowned. "County fairs?"

"I do a little stunt flying for a friend who manages an air acrobatics show. We follow the fairs." He grinned. "You should see me in my getup. Charles Lindbergh all the way."

When Don arched an eyebrow, Tyler shrugged. "There's good money in it."

"Yeah, well, it'd have to be better than just 'good' before you'd catch me doing nosedives over a gawking crowd." Shaking his head in obvious bemusement, Don picked up one last paper plate, which he tossed into his bag. He then perused the room. "Guess that does it. Let me get rid of these bags, and then I'll show you where you're going to sleep."

"Are you sure it's okay if I stay here? I mean, I can find a motel downtown if it's any trouble at all."

"Dad was so thrilled to have you that he's sleeping in one of the spare rooms so you can have the good bed." Don waved away the protest Tyler opened his mouth to make. "Trust me, you'll pay for the comfort. By the time you leave here Dad's going to know every detail of every adventure you've had for the past eight years and then some. He's nosier than an old woman."

"My ex would clobber you if she heard a sexist remark like that," Tyler murmured with a laugh.

Don's jaw dropped. "I didn't know you got married," he murmured, just as Julie exited the kitchen into the living room.

Very aware of her presence, Tyler shrugged. "I used the term loosely. Actually, we just lived together for a while."

"What happened?" Julie asked, crossing the room to set yet another bulging trash bag at her brother's feet.

Tyler gave her a long look. "She started talking weddings," he replied. "We had an agreement, a no-strings setup that worked well, then all at once—" he shook his head, as always mystified by female logic that turned pros into cons. "I'll never figure out what the hell I did to make her think I was ready to tie the knot."

"Of course you won't," Julie interjected rather sharply. "Men and women aren't on the same wavelength."

"What are you talking about?" Tyler asked, a thoughtless question that earned him a what-did-I-tell-you smile from Julie and a wry laugh from Don.

"I'm talking about sexual differences," she replied, rocking back on the heels of her black leather scrunch boots, "and I don't mean the obvious physical ones."

"I kind of like the obvious physical ones," Don interjected, ducking when Julie swatted at him.

"What I'm saying is that women place different meanings on certain things than men do." When Don and Tyler exchanged a baffled glance, Julie sighed. "For example, take your basic, everyday kiss."

Tyler tensed.

"Why do you kiss a woman, Don?" Julie asked.

Her brother grinned. "Several reasons, but mainly because it's a good way to get close enough to explore those obvious physical differences you mentioned."

Julie nodded. "Exactly. To you—and most other men—" she looked pointedly at Tyler "—kisses are nothing more than a lead-in to sex, which, as we all know, is the ultimate male goal."

"And what are kisses to you, er, to women, if I may ask?" Tyler frowned slightly as he waited for her reply.

"A woman considers physical intimacy to be a stepping stone to the ultimate *female* goal, which is commitment."

Tyler winced at her use of the C word—a word thrown at him before, a word he'd come to dread.

Julie, obviously not missing his reaction, lifted her chin and looked down her nose at him. "That's why we take it so personally when someone we consider a possible mate kisses and runs. Now if you two will excuse me, I'm going to bed." That said, she sashayed past the men, leaving in her wake an icy chill that made Tyler shiver.

When they were alone again, Don shook his head. "Don't mind her, Ty. She's always been like that—poking her nose where it doesn't belong, analyzing everyone's motives, handing out free advice." He flashed a grin of mock exasperation. "It drives me nuts sometimes, but what can I do? I'm stuck with her."

Well, I'm not, Tyler thought, renewing his determination to have his say and bring their conflict to closure. Come tomorrow—er, today—they'd talk. He'd finally clear the air once and for all and get on with his life, unhampered by the guilt of old sins and the hard feelings of foolish misunderstandings.

Tyler woke with a start and lay in confusion, heart pounding, unsure of where he was. Something had wakened him...a sound that didn't belong in his apartment.

He frowned into the dark and only gradually recalled the where and why of his current situation. A quick glance round the room confirmed it: Idaho. Julie's house. Tyler glanced at his travel alarm, groaning when he saw the time, 4:30 a.m. He'd slept barely an hour and felt like hell.

What on earth had shattered his dreams? he wondered even as he heard the sound again. Crying. A child's crying. One of brother Sid's crew, no doubt. Perhaps the early bird.

But no, he decided moments later, frowning again. Something was wrong. This cry was one of pain.

At that moment, someone pounded on his door. "Dad? Are you awake?"

In a flash, Tyler stood beside the bed, tugging sweats over the briefs that were all he'd worn to bed since the house was kept so warm. He reached his door just as it opened.

"Dad, I—" Julie gasped. "You! Oh God, I'm sorry. I didn't realize there'd been a switch in rooms." She clutched a pajama-clad toddler against her chest—a boy, Tyler guessed—and jounced him as she spoke. "Where's Dad sleeping?"

"I'm afraid I don't know," Tyler admitted. "Is this Sid's stepson?"

"This is Sid's baby, Josh. He fell out of bed and now he's bleeding from somewhere, but won't let me look to find out where."

Tyler fumbled for the overhead light switch for what seemed an eternity before he found it. He then reached out to catch Julie's elbow and lead her into his room.

"Sit on the bed," he said, a command Julie obeyed with obvious reluctance. Josh sobbed softly, a sound that wrenched Tyler's heart and reduced the child's aunt to near tears, from the look of it.

Tyler dropped to one knee by the bed and touched the boy's shoulder. "Hey, Josh, whasamatter?"

Without releasing his stranglehold on his aunt Julie, the toddler turned his head just enough to identify the speaker. His eyes, huge and dark, brimmed over with tears. Tyler instantly spotted the blood—on the boy's face and on his aunt's filmy pink nightgown—oozing from a jagged cut on the underside of his chin.

"It's coming from a cut—see?—just under his chin, there. We're going to have to wash it off so we can see how bad it is."

"There should be a cloth in the bathroom," Julie replied, pointing to the door that led to the bath just off Tyler's room.

Tyler made short work of finding the cloth and wetting it with warm water. A quick search of the medicine cabinet produced Band-Aids, which he hoped were all he'd need. By the time he returned to the bed, Julie had managed to seat Josh in her lap so that Tyler could see his chin.

She reached for the cloth and Tyler gave it to her. The instant she tried to dab Josh's chin he began to struggle and scream again.

"Let me," Tyler said, taking the cloth back. "Josh. Hey buddy. Look-a here."

Josh, still crying, but clearly curious about Tyler, did as requested.

"That's *great.* Now be a big boy and let me wash you up, okay?"

To Julie's obvious astonishment, Josh again did as asked, struggling only when Tyler touched the actual cut to asses its severity.

"It's not deep," Tyler was finally able to announce. "Just a scratch, really. No stitches required." While he talked, he bandaged, then he used the cloth to clean Josh's hands, Julie's hands and finally her neck—

tender ministrations endured without complaint from child or aunt. Gallantly he kept his gaze above the tips of her breasts, dark shadows under the sheer fabric of her gown. "There, all done. Feeling better?"

The question was directed to Josh, but Julie answered it. "Much, thanks. You're very good at this. Got any little ones of your own?"

"No, thank God," Tyler replied, a candid, but thoughtless, reply that earned him a censorious frown from Julie.

At once she placed a noisy kiss on her nephew's head and hugged him hard—sure indication she valued rug rats much more than Tyler did. She then caught her breath, obviously just realizing that the gown she wore covered everything but hid nothing. Julie raised her gaze to meet Tyler's, her face and neck flushed from forehead to cleavage.

"I've got to leave now..."

Though sorely tempted to argue, Tyler didn't. Instead, he stood back and let her rise. Holding Josh to her chest as before—this time to hide breasts Tyler had once caressed—Julie backed toward the door. Only when she reached it did she spin around, and then just to dash out. She was quick, but not so quick Tyler didn't get a glimpse of skimpy black panties, nearly bare bottom and long, shapely legs.

At once his body responded to the sight. With a groan he fell facedown on the bed, overcome with memories of the taste, smell and feel of her. Was *this,* then, the power she held over him? Sheer sexual thrill? It was a familiar spell, to be sure. One not experienced since the first time they met, eight years ago, but one well remembered all the same. The difference was their ages. She'd been a child then, a hot-to-trot teenager whose kiss had not revealed her innocence, but set him on fire. How did she kiss now that she was grown up and experienced in the ways of love? Tyler dared not try to imagine. If the kiss of a teen could haunt him for eight years, what would the kiss of a woman do?

Tyler groaned again, softly, but from the heart, then crawled back under the covers. Surprisingly he slept, but his dreams were crazy and erotic—the dreams of a man beguiled.

"More bacon?"

"Yes, please."

Standing just outside the kitchen swing door, Tyler listened to the sounds of a family at breakfast. Several emotions washed over him at once, not the least of which was discomfort that surely resulted from the fact that he was the only child of a single parent. Acutely aware of his past experiences with—and subsequent aversion to—large, noisy families, Tyler actually turned to slip back upstairs when the door swung out and hit him in the backside.

"Oomph!" he exclaimed as a small boy charged past him.

"Come on in, Tyler," called John Newman from the kitchen. "There's plenty to eat and a place to sit now that Tim's headed to the den. The Tournament of Roses Parade is on, you know, and he doesn't intend to miss it."

Squaring his shoulders, Tyler pushed through the door into the kitchen filled with family members. Only Kit could not be accounted for. Tyler assumed she was already at work.

John gave him a big smile. "Have a seat. Have a seat."

Tyler skirted the table slowly en route to the proffered chair, nodding an awkward greeting to all who ate and stopping at Josh's high chair to lean down and peer at his bandaged chin. It looked great, he thought, an opinion reaffirmed when Julie spoke.

"He's fine today. Thanks again for helping out."

"No problem," Tyler murmured as he brushed bread crumbs and bits of egg off the chair just vacated by Tim, then sat.

"I want you to know that I don't always do that," Julie said.

"Excuse me?" All Tyler could think of was her sexy nightgown. Did she mean that she sometimes slept naked? he wondered, body stirring at the thought.

"Run to my daddy for help when I get in a tight spot," Julie replied, unaware of the direction his thoughts had taken, but setting him straight all the same. "I'm a big girl except where the kids are concerned. Then I fall apart at the least sign of trouble."

Tyler squirmed to ease the sudden bind of his jeans and faked a smile. "The thought never crossed my mind."

"Here, son," said John, passing Tyler a blue china bowl filled with scrambled eggs, cooked to perfection.

"My mother has a bowl like this," Tyler murmured for lack of anything else to say. "She's a retired nurse, living in Washington state."

"With your dad?" John asked.

Tyler shook his head. "Alone."

"Your dad is dead, then?" Apparently John was every bit as nosy as Don had warned.

"A dead*beat.* One of those guys who'll skip out on a woman without marrying her when she tells him he's going to be a daddy." Tyler noted the looks of sympathy passed between Don and Julie. He also noted that Julie then frowned at her dad in an obvious attempt to shut him up.

It didn't work.

"Sorry to hear that," John said, his tone very matter-of-fact. "His loss, of course."

Tyler shrugged in reply and set down the bowl, now minus a generous helping of the eggs.

"We have sausage and bacon, biscuits and hash browns, too," John then said, clearly oblivious to the tension in the room or the fact that for some reason Tyler had just blurted his deepest, darkest secret. "Eat hearty."

"Thanks," Tyler murmured, his gaze glued to the table before him. In seconds his plate was filled and, to make further foolish confessions impossible, his mouth.

Tyler's illegitimate roots obviously didn't bother John, who appeared bound and determined to discuss them. "Your mother never married anyone else, then?"

Tyler quickly swallowed. "No."

"So you have no brothers or sisters?"

"None."

"Then I guess the Newman household is a culture shock for you, huh?"

"Pretty much, yeah."

"Well, don't let that put you off. Big families are a lot of fun, son, and if you're smart, you'll find yourself a good, fertile woman real soon and get busy making one of your own."

"Da-ad!" Julie scolded, her eyes shooting daggers at her tactless parent.

John looked at her in surprise, clearly clueless. "He'll be glad he did, honey. Why, where would I be now if it weren't for all you kids and grandkids? Alone, that's where. Alone and lonely.'' He pointed a finger at Tyler. ''Your father made a poor choice that I'm sure he now regrets. There's no reason for you to make the same one.''

''No, sir,'' Tyler murmured, a lie. In truth, there were several, not the least of which was that big families gave him the willies. No, not even for old-age companionship would he endure the interference, inconvenience and irritation of them.

Chapter Three

"Are you, um, starting the driving lessons this morning?" blurted Don in an obvious attempt to change the subject. "We have sunshine. We have clear roads."

Tyler exchanged a look with Julie, whose face still glowed pink with embarrassment for her dad's pep talk—another reason Tyler was glad he didn't have a houseful of kin to deal with.

"If that's okay...?" she ventured. "The sooner we begin, the sooner we finish. I don't want you to have to hang around here instead of the slopes. I've heard they're great this year."

"This morning is fine," he assured her, adding, "As for the slopes, I'm on no set schedule this trip, so whenever I get to them is fine."

"Tyler quit his job with Sky Flight," Don told his dad, as if Tyler's comment about schedules had just reminded him of the fact.

John poured himself a cup of steaming black coffee. "That so? Who are you flying for now?" He offered the pot to Tyler.

"Actually, I'm self-employed at the moment. I do some charter work and some crop dusting." Tyler picked up an unused mug so John could fill it.

"He also performs with an air show," Don added. Tyler noted that John seemed impressed by the announcement. Julie, however, appeared a bit stunned. Thankfully, talk turned to general topics after that. Tyler, no longer the subject of conversation, thank God, perused everyone at the table, beginning with a blond-haired girl who had to be Sid's other stepchild. Petite, obviously shy, she sat to the right of her step-grandfather, John, who smiled down at her every few seconds.

Without a doubt John was the type of person who thrived on the chaos of a large family. Tyler didn't remember the late Mrs. Newman all that well since he'd only met her once, but he carried in his mind an impression of warmth and motherly patience. He guessed that her loss was probably the reason John had called his family back home.

To the little girl's right—was her name Celia? No, Carly—sat Don, complete with bloodshot eyes and unshaven face. One beer too many? Tyler wondered, instantly excusing the overindulgence. New Year's Eve came just once a year. Tyler knew from experience that Don was a health nut who never drank anything stronger than beer and then only on special occasions such as little sis's birthday party.

And speaking of little sis...she sat a high chair away from Don, at the end of the table across from her dad and to Tyler's left. She looked beautiful this morning, he thought, none the worse for a night of drama.

With her hair pulled back in a ponytail and wearing a tattered sweatshirt, she could easily have been sixteen almost seventeen, just as she was the day they met. That reminded Tyler of his mission, and noting that she'd finished eating, he made short work of cleaning his plate, too.

"Carly and I will take care of the kitchen," John said, when Julie stood from the table, moments after Don excused himself and ran off to get ready for his salespeople, and carried her plate to the sink. "You get started on those driving lessons."

"But—"

"Don't argue." He waved his hands as though to shoo them out. With a shrug, Julie met Tyler at the door, through which they exited.

"My jacket's in the coat closet. Where's yours?" she asked.

"On that hook there." Tyler pointed to a rack near the front door on which hung his leather jacket. Since the closet was nearby, they walked together.

"Shall we?" Julie murmured after she'd donned a denim jacket, inclining her head in the direction of the door that led to the garage. Tyler led the way, opening the door and then stepping back so Julie could pass through it into the garage. Moments later found them peering under the hood of the Corvette—a dream car in Tyler's opinion.

"I just want to learn to clutch and shift this thing," Julie grumbled when Tyler automatically reached for the dip stick. "I already know how to check the oil."

"Oh, um, right." He walked round to the passenger side, pausing only to flick a speck of dust off the gleaming vehicle. Then he opened the door and settled into the white leather bucket seat, where he sat long moments in reverent silence.

Man, oh man, what a car. Classic. Immaculate. Sexy as—

"Tyler!"

Tyler started and glanced over at Julie, now seated behind the wheel and looking a bit impatient.

"Could we please get on with this?"

"Sorry." He gave the instrument panel a quick once-over. "First, you should familiarize yourself with everything," he said, and then enthusiastically explained each button, gauge and switch as well as the workings of the transmission. He showed her not only the location of each gear, but how to shift without stripping them. "There now. Any questions?" For the first time in several minutes, he dragged his gaze from the stick shift to Julie.

Her eyes twinkled with what could only be amusement. Clearly, she struggled not to laugh.

"What?" he asked, baffled by her mirth. "What?"

"Driving this car would almost be a religious experience for you, wouldn't it?"

"Religious? Nah. More... orgasmic."

Julie first gasped at his candid admission, then bubbled with laughter. "Oh, I get it, like eating chocolate is for me."

Still laughing, she started the car. With Tyler directing every move, she backed flawlessly out of the drive. He guessed then she would be a quick study, a fact proved true over the next half hour. At that point Tyler silently acknowledged that another driving lesson might not be necessary. She needed practice, of course, but she'd grasped the basics, there was no denying that. That meant he'd better say what he'd come to say.

"Want a tour of the city?" she asked as if on cue, tossing a bright smile his way. The expression seemed to say that all was forgotten, a phenomenon he credited to their early-morning adventure. The need for explanation had clearly been negated, but Tyler didn't take the out.

"If you can drive and listen at the same time," Tyler responded. "I still haven't explained about—"

"It's not necessary." Her tone of voice belied her words and told him that maybe all wasn't forgotten... just temporarily forgiven.

"Yes, it is."

"No it isn't."

"It is!" The words were almost a shout. Tyler made himself take a deep, steadying breath and tried again. "It is."

"All right, then, tell me... why did you run away? Was it because I was little sister of a friend? That can be awkward, I know."

Tyler sighed. "That's not why."

"Oh? Well, was it—where *is* second gear?—because I didn't have enough, um, chest to suit you. I was a late bloomer."

"Dammit, Julie, *no!*"

"Then why, Tyler? Why'd you leave and never come back to my party. I waited, you know. Waited and watched for you. I even delayed blowing out the candles on that big ol' cake, hoping you'd show up and help me."

Tyler heard the hurt in her voice and winced, hating himself for what he'd done. But he'd had no choice... none at all.

"I left because you were seventeen, and I was twenty-six."

Julie slowed the car and turned into a deserted parking lot, where she killed the engine and turned to look at Tyler, her eyes narrowed. "What do you mean...twenty-six? You were Don's age—twenty-three."

"I think I know how old I am, Julie."

"But he said you were a classmate."

"I was. Some of the hours I took at Washington State didn't transfer to the University of Nevada. I had to repeat a required history course and six additional hours. I was a senior, but I was older than most other seniors, thanks to my having laid out a couple of years, then going only part-time some of the time, so I could indulge my daredevil streak. You know, drive a race car, get my pilot's licence, learn to sky dive...that type of stuff." He reached out and covered her hand, which still clutched the stick shift. "Do you see now why I had to leave?"

"Oh, I see *that,* all right," she told him, shaking off his touch. "What I don't see is why our little encounter ever happened in the first place. Not to mention why you flirted with me all evening."

"Actually, we flirted with each other, but the point is moot. We, um, did what we did, after which I saw your birthday cake and realized you weren't the older sister at all, but jailbait with a capital *J.* Of course, I flew the coop."

"Now just a darn minute. Are you telling me you didn't know how young I was?"

"Of course I didn't know!" Tyler exclaimed, aghast. "If I had, do you think I'd have kissed you, touched you? God, Julie—"

"But we talked about the birthday party all night—"

"And never once mentioned *which one it was* for you." He shook his head. "Don said he had two sisters. Kit was such a fluff I thought she was the baby. He told me it's happened before."

"Even if I had been the older sister I'd have been too young for you."

"Are you saying what happened was my fault?"

She nodded. "Totally."

"Excuse me, but I've always respected the word *no,* and I don't recall hearing it that night. In fact, it was green light all the way."

Julie caught her breath. "That's a lie."

"The hell it is. You wanted me as much as I wanted you."

"I was a child."

"You were a teenager playing with fire, that's what you were. Even if I'd only been twenty-three, I'd still have been too old for you. And you know it."

"All right...all right. So maybe I was a little flattered by the attention, but—" Julie suddenly clamped her mouth shut as if biting back the rest of whatever she was going to say. "Obviously we'll never agree on this, and that's okay because after today, we'll never see each other again. Now can we please go home?"

"You're the driver," Tyler snapped, settling back into the seat, arms folded over the seat belt strap that crossed his chest.

Julie started the engine, then struggled for several minutes to put the car in gear, all driving lessons apparently forgotten in the wake of her irritation with Tyler. He watched without comment and without offering help. If she wanted any, she'd just have to ask for it.

And ask she did.

"Tyler! Are you going to just sit there like an idiot or are you going to put this damned car in gear for me?"

"Can you manage a *please?*" he retorted.

"Please," she said, looking for all the world as if the word choked her.

Calmly Tyler found first gear. Julie promptly stomped the accelerator, resulting in a lurching of the Corvette that threatened his neck with whiplash. In hostile silence they drove back to the house, got out of the sleek red vehicle and headed to the door that connected the garage to the rest of the structure.

Julie's brother and father met them there.

"How'd the lesson go?" Don asked.

"She passed," Tyler replied when Julie didn't. "And that means it's time for me to hit the road."

"Oh, not yet," John said, much to Tyler's surprise. "I want to talk to you first. Don and I both do."

Now what? Tyler wondered, glancing from one man to the other. Reluctantly he let them lead him on into the living room, where Josh sat on the floor, busy with building blocks. When Julie started toward the stairs, John caught her hand and tugged her back in the direction of the fireplace with a brisk "This concerns you, too," that appeared to baffle her as much as it did Tyler.

Quite curious by now, he settled himself on one end of the couch. Don took on the other, and Julie sat on the floor beside Josh. John, clearly in charge, chose a corduroy recliner. In the background Tyler heard the clamor of the television and guessed Carly and Tim watched it in the den.

"Don and I have been talking, Tyler, and we now have a business proposition for you." John smiled. "We want you to be the pilot for New-Ware Manufacturing."

"But you don't have an airplane," Julie said, clearly puzzled.

"Oh, yes I do," John told her. "As of Christmas. My, um, gift to myself."

"You never mentioned it." Her eyes were huge, accusing.

"Didn't I?" John cleared his throat and looked away, obviously uncomfortable. "Must have slipped my mind."

"What kind did you buy?" Tyler asked.

"A 36 Bonanza."

"Good choice." From experience, Tyler knew that the single-engine, four- to six-seater would serve John well.

John beamed like a proud papa. "It's a beaut. So...what do you say? Want a job with New-Ware? We've got great insurance, flexible hours, retirement benefits."

Still a bit taken aback, Tyler hesitated. "I don't know...."

"Plus," John quickly continued, "you'll have enough free days that you can still do whatever crop dusting or other charter work will satisfy your yen for adventure. Believe me, I understand that and don't intend to cramp your style."

"Sounds too good to be true," Tyler murmured, highly conscious of Julie's disapproval and wondering at the depth of it. Did she dislike him *that* much? Or was something else going on? "I'd like to know a little more about what the job entails."

"So would I," Julie said. Tyler did not miss the sarcasm in her voice.

"I'll handle this one, Dad," Don interjected with a grin. "PR is my department, after all." He turned to Tyler. "Are you aware that New-Ware has factories in three states now?"

Tyler shook his head.

"Well, we do—Idaho, Montana, where, as you know, I live, and Nevada. We're trying to expand nationally and even internationally. As a result, Dad, Sid and I travel, as does Julie, who demonstrates our product at better department stores all over the western half of the United States. Up until now, we've flown commercial, which often necessitates overnight stays and results in considerable expense and time away from home. It didn't take a genius to realize Dad could save money if he bought his own small plane and kept his own pilot on call. He and I want that pilot to be you."

Tyler sat in silence a moment, digesting all that he'd heard. It was almost too pat—the kind of situation one saw in the movies. Some pilot needs a new job. Some company needs a pilot. Miraculously they stumble onto one another....

Fate?

"I'd like to think on this, if I may."

"By all means," John said. "And you can stay right here with us until you make up your mind."

"I wouldn't dream of imposing on you another night," Tyler murmured, certain he'd never be able to reach a decision surrounded by Newman kith and kin.

"Why, it's no imposition at all. In fact, your staying over will just make it easier for me to take you to the plant and the airport tomor—"

"But he came to *ski,* Dad," Julie interrupted, now visibly upset—too upset, in Tyler's opinion.

"Hell, honey, if he moves to Clear Falls he can ski whenever he wants!" John stood to give Tyler an enthusiastic slap on the back.

Thanking his lucky stars that his sweater was thick and took most of the hearty blow, Tyler smiled at the old man, an expression which must have further irritated Julie. At any rate she leapt to her feet, scooped Josh up into her arms and stalked to the stairs, actions her sibling and parent didn't seem to notice.

"The Clear Falls airport is small, but adequate—"

"We'll pay top dollar—"

Tyler held up a hand, halting their rush of words. "I repeat—I'm flattered," he said. "I'm also a little overwhelmed, so if you don't mind, I think I'll go up to my room and give this proposition time to soak in."

"Oh, sure. Fine. Didn't mean to rush you," John said, looking a bit sheepish.

With a nod at both John and his son, Tyler headed for the stairs himself. He took them two at a time and then marched down the hall to the room he guessed must be Julie's, judging from the source of Josh's crying earlier that morning.

He knocked on the door, waited half a second, then knocked louder.

"I'm coming. I'm coming." It was Julie, all right, and she sounded more than a little put out. Her expression upon opening the door confirmed it. "What do *you* want?"

"Can we talk?"

"Again?"

"It's important," Tyler told her, by now a little irritated himself. Something about the stubborn set of her chin brought out the worst in him for sure.

"The job, I suppose." Julie sighed. "Look, Tyler. I don't mean to sound like a grump, but I really don't approve of the fact that Dad bought a plane."

"Why not?"

"Because he has no business with one."

"But he'll save his company money."

"As if that really had anything to do with it."

Baffled, Tyler stood in silence for a moment. "May I come in?"

"Why?"

"Because there's something going on here that I don't understand, and I need to know what it is before I make a decision on this job."

Julie's first reaction was to shake her head, then she seemed to think twice and actually opened the door wide. Stepping aside, she motioned him into the room.

It was huge, Tyler realized, almost an apartment—an *ultrafeminine* apartment, thanks to the eyelet, ruffles and lace everywhere. Tyler noticed that there was no baby bed. Had Josh, then, slept with his aunt last night?

Lucky kid.

Tyler spied an overflowing toy box and a rocking horse. In arm's reach of it sat Josh, dressed in overalls, a red-striped T-shirt and the tiniest shoes Tyler had ever seen. When he spotted the word Weeboks on them, he grinned, charmed.

"Hi, buddy," Tyler said and then walked over to kneel by the child, who played with a fire truck that made motor noises and flashed its lights every time he rolled it across the hardwood floor.

Josh gave him a look, but said nothing.

"Let's sit here," Julie said, pointing to a window seat big enough for two.

With a nod Tyler rose and joined her there. They sat, knees brushing, an oddly intimate sensation. "Okay. What's the problem? Is it me? Do you dislike me so much that you'd be miserable if I took the job?"

"I don't dislike you, Tyler." She seemed almost startled by the idea.

"You could've fooled me," he murmured.

Julie frowned. "You really thought that?"

"Of course I did. We've been fighting since I walked in the door last night...er, this morning. What else was I supposed to think?"

"I guess I *have* been rude, haven't I?" She shook her head. "I don't know why, exactly. Maybe seeing you again put me back in some teenaged mode or something...."

"Threw me back in time, too," Tyler admitted. "But you're not a teenager anymore."

"No, I'm not, and I'm sorry for acting as if I were. I like you just fine, Tyler, and I thank you for helping me with Josh this morning and for the driving lesson. If I've hurt your feelings in any way, I apologize." She gave him a smile that didn't quite reach her eyes. "Forgive me?"

"Of course," he said. "And just for the record, I like you, too. What a shame we got off on such a bad start. I mean, who knows what might have happened if we'd met for the first time at this year's party. Why, we might actually have—"

Placing a forefinger on his lips, Julie silenced him. "All I said was that I liked you, Tyler. I didn't say I was interested in dating you. I certainly didn't say I wanted you, okay?"

Put firmly in his place, Tyler could only nod.

"Now about this stupid plane—"

"You don't like to fly, I take it."

"I like flying fine—if I'm sitting in a plane that holds a hundred people."

"So it's just smaller planes that scare you?"

"Actually, I've never even been on one, and if Dad had any sense, he'd avoid them, too. But no—" she rolled her eyes in utter disgust "—for years now, he's wanted to buy a single- or twin-engine plane and learn to fly it. Mother wouldn't hear of it, of course, since one of her brothers died in a plane crash during the Korean War. Then Cord's plane went down...." Her voice trailed to silence. She sighed and looked away.

So that's it. Cord had died in a plane crash, not on a jump as Tyler had assumed. He watched Julie closely. She blinked a few times and swallowed hard, clearly struggling with her emotion. Several seconds of silence passed before she turned her gaze on Tyler again. "You'd think Dad would realize how dangerous small planes are, but what does he do? Buy one of his own. Learning to fly it will be next, of course, and he's too old. Just too old."

"Exactly how old are we talking, here?"

"Fifty-eight."

"You call that old?"

"I knew it! I knew it!" Julie leapt to her feet. "You think the plane is a good idea, don't you?"

"I *am* a pilot, Julie."

"A pilot who will soon be hit up for flying lessons, I expect. And you, by golly, will probably give them to him."

"I might...."

Julie huffed her outrage. "See? You want to know why I'm upset? *That's* why I'm upset." She walked over to one of the other windows, where she stood looking out, hugging herself like a little lost girl.

Tyler stood and walked up behind her. Gently he clasped her shoulders and forced a turn until she faced him again. "I understand how worried you are, and I understand why. But are you really going to deny your father his dream?"

"You bet I am, mister!"

"Every man has a right to adventure. Every woman does, too, for that matter. I'll bet your dad has supported you in whatever you've decided to do...even living in Alaska, which must have been hell for him."

Julie wilted right before Tyler's eyes. "Oh God. You're right, of course. Mother said he cried like a baby *after* I got on the plane. Before, well, he acted so proud." To Tyler's dismay her eyes filled with tears. "I just can't bear the thought of the risk. Cord is gone. And my mother, too—"

Without thought, Tyler reached out and tugged Julie into his arms. He hugged her hard, an action that was more reflex than anything else, and though she stood stiffly in the embrace at first, she soon relaxed against him.

Body to body, they stood. Tyler cherished the unexpected closeness—the smell and feel of her that was so familiar. At once, it was eight years ago and he held the beautiful young sister of a friend out on their deck. As he had that fateful night, he experienced a rush of wonder and desire, an anticipation of good things to come.

Ever so gingerly, he lowered his head to brush his cheek against her hair, soft as silk. Julie tensed again and tipped her head back to look at him. Their gazes locked. Tyler felt her heart begin to thud erratically... or was it his own?

His gaze dropped to her mouth, so inviting. He wanted like crazy to kiss her, just as he had so long ago. Would she let him? he wondered, even as she moistened her lips with a nervous flick of her tongue. He swallowed hard, struggling to resist temptation.

"Dada!"

Both started at the sound of Josh's cry. Tyler looked down and found the child standing at his feet, clutching a handful of his khaki pants, about knee-high.

"Did he just call me Dada?" Tyler asked, even as Julie slipped free of his embrace and ended all hopes of a kiss.

"He did not." She picked up her nephew and hugged him.

"But he did. He called me Dada." Tyler considered the word *Dada* and all its ramifications—long-term commitment, lifelong dedication, eternal love. He shuddered. Such did not tempt Tyler Jordan, though he had to admit the kid was cute.

"What he said was *Band-Aid.* His grampa bought him some with dinosaurs on them today. I understand he's been through six already." Julie looked down at her nephew. "You want another Band-Aid on your chin?"

Josh shook his head. "Dada." He reached for Tyler, chubby fists clenching and unclenching in his eagerness to be taken.

With a smug smile Tyler held out his arms for Josh, who struggled to get away from his aunt. Frowning slightly, Julie let him go to Tyler.

"I'm Ty," Tyler said to Josh. "Can you say 'Ty'?"

"Dada."

"Do you suppose he thinks I'm his daddy?" Tyler asked when Josh then gave him a choking hug and an open-mouthed, slightly sticky baby kiss on the cheek.

"Don't be ridiculous," Julie snapped. "He waved bye-bye to his daddy less than two weeks ago. He couldn't have forgotten him that quick."

Tyler shrugged and turned away from her, heading to the window seat. He settled himself on it, then let Josh stand on his lap. "Maybe I remind him of his dad or something. What color is Sid's hair?"

"Brown, like yours."

"And his eyes?"

"They're brown, too."

"Then that's it. I remind Josh of his dad. I'm sure the little guy misses him."

"Poor baby," Julie murmured, clearly troubled by the idea that Josh might confuse Tyler with her oldest brother, who would be gone for weeks yet.

"Actually, I think he's got it made in the shade." Tyler grinned at Josh, who grinned back and laughed. "If Rita could see me now."

"Rita?"

"The woman I lived with. The one who wanted commitment in the form of wedding bells and babies." God forbid.

"Oh, *her.*" Julie gave Tyler a thoughtful look, then joined him on the window seat. "How long were you two together?"

"Long enough." Tyler hated answering personal questions so was a bit short in his determination to discourage any others. Without response, Julie got abruptly to her feet and began to pick up the toys scattered around the room, her movements quick and agitated.

At once Tyler regretted his impatient tone of voice...or was she still upset about the job offer? Guessing the latter, Tyler reminded himself that Julie was entitled to her opinion about flying, after all, and certainly had justification for it.

But what if that wasn't the problem, either? What if she found his presence in her room, and maybe in her house, more upsetting than the flying or even his reluctance to share details about his love life?

"Just so you know," he murmured on impulse, "I'm not going to hang around here until I make up my mind about this job. I really did come to Idaho to ski in a downhill race."

"Not the GR?" Her censorious gaze nailed him to the wall.

Tyler ignored it. "That's the one. So you see I haven't got time to hang around chit-chatting with you guys."

"Too bad," she murmured so sweetly that he knew she lied. Her relief that he was leaving gave him his answer. It also raised another question: if Julie really didn't dislike him, then why did she care if he hung around for a while?

Chapter Four

A short time later Julie sat alone in her room with Josh. She had shut the door behind Tyler with a sigh of relief. He made her nervous, there was no denying that. Why, she couldn't imagine. He was nothing more than a loose end finally tied. If anything, she should be relaxed and carefree around him. Instead, she was moody and emotional—a hormonal horror story.

Were his dashing good looks to blame? she wondered, as she pulled a very grumpy Josh's shoes from his feet and then tucked him into the bed for a midmorning snooze. Or was it the way his gaze dropped to her mouth or her breasts every time they talked? Julie found the habit very disconcerting. It made her wonder if he wanted to kiss her, touch her.

In truth, Julie wanted to kiss and touch *him*... but only to see how it would feel this time around. Their last contact of that kind was so long ago. They'd both changed... or had they? Though somewhat older in appearance—new laugh lines, the occasional silver hair—Tyler was still nothing more than a devil-may-care charmer. And she...well, she was still a hopeless romantic, a heroine too easily beguiled by the rakish hero.

That's what drew her first to Tyler at seventeen and then to Cord at twenty. That's what kept her from playing the dating game now. Julie had long ago recognized her penchant for men who walked on the wild side and, sadder but wiser about life with them, intended to proceed with caution.

Caution? Julie wanted to laugh.

Could kissing or touching Tyler—even for purposes of experimentation—ever be considered the action of a cautious woman? Julie wondered. Only, she decided, if she was the *experimenter* and not the experiment.

Julie sat on the bed beside her nephew and grinned, suddenly assailed with a vision of herself in a spotless white lab coat, standing next to Tyler, who was strapped in a throne-type chair. Next to him were similar chairs, on which were strapped other men, all of *them* strangers. Julie, clipboard in hand, walked to each in turn and kissed them soundly on the mouth, then scribbled notes on her paper.

She imagined what she would write about Tyler. Lips—firm, yet sensuous. Breath—mint scented.

"Yum."

Tongue—skilled.

"Yum. Yum."

Overall score—9.5 out of 10, not bad for an eight-year-old memory. And that was only the kissing part of the experiment. Just wait until she got her hands on that hot body of his.

"JuJu! Yum!"

With a guilty start, Julie snapped out of her Technicolor fantasy and looked down at her nephew, who pointed impatiently to the box of cookies, called Yums, that she kept on a shelf by the bed they'd been sharing. She immediately stood and reached for it.

"So you're hungry, huh? Well, apparently so am I, but not for food." She sighed—a wistful sound even to her own ears. "I think what I'm hungry for is change or maybe excitement or challenge or something. I don't know. What I'm *not* hungry for is Tyler Jordan's kisses or—"

"More."

"That's right, Josh. I'm not hungry for anything *more* he has to give, either, nor am I depressed about his leaving." She handed Josh a second cookie, which he immediately stuck in his mouth, then absently nibbled one herself.

"No," Josh said, reaching for her half-eaten cookie and shaking his head so hard his hair stood on end.

"You don't believe me?" Julie handed him a third Yum. "It's really the truth. Tyler Jordan does not ring my chimes—" she frowned at Josh "—that's slang, honey. It means Tyler doesn't, um, excite me. Well, maybe *excite* isn't exactly the right word. My heart rate *does* triple whenever he's around, Lord knows why. How can I put this?" She thought for a moment. "I know. Tyler doesn't make me forget where and who I am. Therefore, I've got my goals firmly in mind, which is where they will stay." She tousled Josh's hair. "Now what do you think of that?"

"Buh."

"Did you say...*bull?*" Julie stared in disbelief at the baby genius.

Josh gave her a solemn nod. "Buh." He pointed to the floor, where lay the stuffed moose that Don had dubbed Bullwinkle.

Laughing at herself—Josh might be a good conversationalist one day, but not yet—Julie scooped up the moose and handed it to her nephew. She then put up the cookies and walked over to the window.

"Josh, honey, look!" she exclaimed on glancing outside. Hurrying back to get him, she scooped the toddler out of the bed and returned to the window so she could point out the snowflakes, big as silver dollars, now sifting to the ground. "Look at the snow. Isn't it pretty?"

Josh watched in fascination for a moment, then laughed with delight—a cherub Julie adored. Overcome with love, she hugged him so tightly he began to squirm and protest. Reluctantly she put him back into bed and then returned to the window seat, where she sat and wished with all her heart for a house and a child of her own.

Of course she'd need to find herself a husband first—one with an ordinary desk job that left his weekends free. Unfortunately Julie didn't even have a boyfriend at the moment.

Down below a door slammed, and Julie heard voices outside. Pressing her face to the window, she peered out and saw both Don and Tyler headed down the sidewalk to their vehicles.

So Tyler was leaving, too. Good.

At once the house seemed to close in and the silence became ominous. Irritated with her sudden blue mood, she sternly reminded herself that even if Tyler's laughter didn't echo throughout, even if she wouldn't meet him on the stair, this house was still wonderfully warm and secure, still home.

And those who shared it with her—John, Kit, Sid's crew, and sometimes Don—they were all she really needed to be happy.

Weren't they?

The next week, vacation time for Julie, passed quickly—a blur of activities ranging from buying a new cookbook to practicing her driving. The result of the new cookbook was a Saturday dinner that featured several tasty new dishes developed especially for the cooking demonstrations that would resume on Monday. The result of all the driving was new confidence and a sense of accomplishment that did much to lift Julie's spirits.

Sunday morning, Julie drove Don to the airport, a favor that usually depressed her. Still emotionally up, however, she successfully fought off her blues, and the afternoon found her able to laugh at the antics of Joshua, Tim and Carly, tumbling on the den carpet in mimicry of the gymnasts competing on television. Kit stood with video camera in hand and caught their tricks, stopping now and then when her laughter compromised the quality of the film.

Neither heard the doorbell ring until their father yelled from his office in the back of the house for one of them to answer it. Julie immediately jumped up and ran. She found Tyler standing on the porch, a Stetson hat, of all things, in hand.

"Hi," he said with a smile. "How've you been?"

"Fine, thanks." Julie allowed herself one quick once-over of their visitor, noting that today he wore a suede jacket with sheepskin lining, Western-style shirt, jeans and boots. Lord, what a specimen! "How about you? Did you win your race?"

"Nah. I crashed about midway down the slope."

Julie gasped.

"Oh, I'm all right. Just banged up my knee a little."

"Lucky you," Julie murmured, her tone admittedly sarcastic. "Um, come on in."

Tyler stepped into the foyer. "Is your dad home?"

So this was it. The moment of truth. Julie swallowed hard.

"He's in his office. Follow me." She led the way down the hall, passing the door to the living room and the den en route. Kit called out a greeting to Tyler as they passed.

"In here," Julie said, when they reached John Newman's office. She ushered Tyler in, listened to three seconds' worth of small talk, then quietly slipped outside, halting just outside the door where eavesdropping was possible.

"I've thought about your job offer all week," Julie heard Tyler say. "And if you still want me, I'm yours."

"Of course I still want you!" John Newman gushed, even as Julie sagged against the wall. Silently she made her way back to the den.

"Good grief," Kit murmured, glancing up from her camera. "Who died?"

"No one," Julie admitted and then explained. "Tyler's taking the pilot job."

"Oh, good."

Julie gave her sister a long look. "Good? You agree with this airplane business?"

"Well, I'm not as much against it as you are," Kit replied. "But then I didn't lose my husband in a crash." She thought for a moment before speaking again. "I guess I'm okay with this because I know that Dad is not going to change his mind. The way I see it, if members of my family are going to put their lives in the hands of a pilot, I'd much rather they chose the best one around."

"And you think Tyler's the best one around?"

"Frankly, I don't know anything about it, but Don sure believes in him."

"Then I guess I should take my cue from big bro," Julie commented, and let the matter drop. She had no intentions of explaining that there were other issues involved, other reasons she'd hoped Tyler would turn down the job. Kit would never understand them. Julie didn't herself.

Something—she didn't know what—made his employment an event to dread. Was it what had happened between them eight years ago? Was it their arguments earlier that week? Neither meant anything, and Julie really knew it.

So why this fluttery feeling in the pit of her stomach? Why these sweaty palms? These weak knees? As sensible as her heart was these days, surely those physical reactions couldn't result from any fear that she couldn't resist his charms.

At the front of the house, a door opened, then closed.

"Julie, Kit...where are you two?" It was John, his voice trembling with excitement.

"In the den." Julie faked a smile when he burst into the room alone.

"Tyler has accepted our offer. We've got ourselves a pilot!" He scooped up Josh and danced an impromptu jig, producing peals of laughter from his grandchildren and Kit.

Julie, helpless to resist the joyful sound, found herself laughing, too. If Tyler's taking this job could make her dad this happy, then she guessed she could live with the idea. She'd only have to be with him a couple of days a week, after all. That was honestly no big deal.

"When does he start?" she asked.

"Monday."

"So soon?" Kit asked. "Shouldn't you give him time to find an apartment and get settled in?"

John shook his head. "No need. I talked him into staying with us until he gets to know the area well enough to make an informed decision about permanent housing. Motels are so expensive this time of year—he's already spent a week in one—and there's not a vacant apartment in the city."

"Oh, Dad, you didn't!" Julie groaned.

John's smile instantly vanished. "You don't want him to stay with us?"

"Feeding family is one thing," Julie told him for lack of a better explanation, her gut positively churning now. "Feeding a guest is something else. You know that I don't always have time to cook a real meal."

John chuckled, clearly relieved, and waved away her feeble protest. "If you served canned soup every night, he wouldn't complain. In fact, living here should be a treat for him. From the sound of things he's been soloing it in a Yakima, Washington, apartment for years. In fact, he told me that everything he owns can be stuffed in boxes and loaded on the New-Ware plane Thursday when he flies you to Yakima for your demonstration there." John stood and glanced at his watch. "Now he'll be back in a couple of hours. Think you can have a room ready for him by then?"

With a sigh of resignation, Julie nodded. "I suppose you're putting him on the third floor?" There was a big room up there, adjacent to the one Sid's stepchildren occupied.

"Next to Carly and Tim? I wouldn't do that to my worst enemy. No, I want you to put him in Don's room. I'm sure he won't mind sharing a bath with you."

"Da-ad!"

"A bath*room,* I mean," John managed to amend, before dissolving into raucous, knee-slapping laughter.

It was at that moment that Julie finally realized just why she dreaded Tyler's working at New-Ware. The purchase of the plane or the hiring of Tyler to pilot it wasn't what tied her stomach in knots, though those were bad enough.

No, it was John's treating Tyler like family and expecting—even demanding—that everyone else do the same.

Try as she might, Julie could not think of Tyler as a brother or even a distant cousin. The feelings she harbored for him were different...shockingly different. So shockingly different, in fact, that just the thought of his showering or shaving one wall away was enough to set her sensible ol' heart to hammering.

Tyler returned to the house later Sunday evening. The moment her dad opened the front door, Julie knew without looking who had arrived—not a good omen. Was she so finely tuned to him that the very beat of her heart acted as a sort of Geiger counter, thumping wildly at his approach?

Distressed by the idea, Julie almost refused her dad's prompt to show Tyler his room. And during the climb upstairs, the silence between them grew so long and awkward that Julie actually jumped when Tyler finally broke it.

"I hope my staying here isn't too much of an inconvenience. Your dad just wouldn't take no for an answer."

Julie sighed in response, well acquainted with dear John's stubbornness. "I'm okay with it. I just hope we don't drive you nuts. A big family such as ours can be a bit overwhelming when you're not used to them."

"Maybe just a bit," he murmured, his expression guarded.

When he said nothing else, Julie sighed again, oddly disappointed that he hadn't argued with her or at least predicted he'd soon get used to the Newman clan. The next instant she wondered at her disappointment. Surely she wasn't harboring some secret notion of taming this guy. Hadn't her rocky marriage to Cord—a man with Tyler's yen for high adventure—taught her anything about false optimism and the cold, hard facts of life?

When they reached the top of the stairs, Julie led the way to the room that would be Tyler's—Don's usual sleeping quarters whenever he was home. Tyler took a quick look around the spacious area, furnished in maroon and hunter green with lots of wood trim, and nodded his pleasure. At once Julie felt a rush of pleasure all her own. Obviously he liked this bedroom that she had redecorated herself not so long ago.

But why she cared what he thought, Julie couldn't say.

"We'll share the bathroom," she told Tyler, pointing out the room, also recently redone. It had two doors, one that opened into Tyler's room and one that opened into Julie's. "We'll have to choreograph bath time, I guess. Do you prefer morning or night?"

"Morning, but I'm flexible."

"Morning's great, actually. I prefer night." Absently she added, "One of my favorite sensations is that of clean skin and hair against clean sheets."

"I have a favorite sensation, too," Tyler commented, words that made Julie tense. She could well imagine what X-rated thrill that might be.

"Oh?"

"That little tickle I get in my gut when I'm flying my plane upside down."

"Oh." So the sensation wasn't sexual after all. She should've known he'd rate the thrill of danger above any other. Cord all over again. Suddenly depressed, Julie changed the subject. "There's a washer and dryer in the basement that you're welcome to use anytime and a clothesline in the backyard, should you prefer the smell of fresh air over that of fabric softener."

"I've avoided clotheslines since I ran into one riding a moped." He tipped back his head to show her a scar just under his chin.

"It's a good thing your mother was a nurse," she responded, a little sick to her stomach.

Tyler laughed at that.

Not nearly as amused, Julie glanced quickly around the room, searching for something to say to this crazy man. "Er... any questions about anything?"

"No. How about you? Any questions?"

"What kind would I have?" she asked.

"Oh... questions about me, my life-style. We're going to be sharing a roof, after all. Surely you're wondering if I stay up late, get up early, jog, sing in the shower or snore?"

"Sharing a roof with you will be no different from our both being guests at a bed and breakfast somewhere, Tyler," Julie told him with a toss of her hair. "We'll remain near strangers, living lives that intersect only when there's a chance passing on the stairs, a meeting in the living room or a shared meal."

"I...see."

Did he sound disappointed? But of course not...and even if he'd been hoping for more, that was just too bad. Julie had no intentions of adopting Tyler Jordan. Well aware of Cupid's knack for preying on unsuspecting hearts, she knew she must do her level best to avoid emotional entanglement with this attractive man so opposite to the man of her dreams. Why, if she let down her guard for a moment when around Tyler, Cupid might swoop in, draw that damned bow of his and fire at the two of them.

Julie shuddered at the thought and with a hasty excuse, left Tyler alone in his room. She headed straight to the kitchen and busied herself with dinner, therapy that always lightened blue moods since it took her mind off her problems.

Less than an hour later Julie summoned everyone to the table for a meal of homemade pizza—the kids' favorite. When Tyler answered the call, but declined to dine, she thought to clarify the issue of mealtimes.

"You do know you're welcome to eat with us," she told him as she settled Josh into the high chair. John, already seated and placing a napkin in Carly's lap, nodded agreement.

"Your dad made that clear, and I'm grateful for your generosity. I stopped for a burger on my way over here, though, so I'm not hungry tonight."

"Hmm. Well, I'd appreciate knowing when you're going to eat...just so I'll have enough," Julie told him as she handed Tim a glass of chocolate milk.

Tyler, now leaning negligently against the doorjamb, hands in his pockets, shook his head. "You don't have to cook extra just for me."

"It's really no problem," she said and then sat between Tim and Josh. Don's and Kit's chairs stood empty since he was back in Montana and she was still at the hospital. "If you'll just let me know your schedule."

"Yes, ma'am," Tyler murmured much to John's amusement. "But I don't expect to eat here without contributing to the grocery bill. I'll even help you cook."

John grinned at that. "You cook?"

"Some things."

"Don't tell me, let me guess," Julie said. "Spaghetti, chili, bacon and eggs—"

"Actually, I cook a mean pot roast, and I'm not half-bad with fried chicken."

Julie blinked in surprise. Now this was domestication she hadn't expected from a wild man... darn him. "I'm impressed."

"You really will be when you taste them."

John, clearly enjoying their banter, seemed to have forgotten the reason he sat at the table. Irritated, Julie pointed to the food, which grew cool. Her dad nodded, helped the two oldest grandkids to a slice, then helped himself.

Julie cut up tiny bites for Josh, who had just enough teeth to gnaw them, then ate her own pizza without another glance at the door. When she finally did risk a peek in that direction, Tyler was long gone. She relaxed at once, comfortable with those who sat at the table—family members she loved and cherished in a way she suspected Tyler never could.

The irony of her thoughts was not lost on Julie, who marveled that whenever she let her mind dwell on Tyler, she found herself ranking him not as a possible date, but as a possible mate. One look at him and she instantly pondered marriage issues such as family acceptance, mutual decorating tastes, sex and lifelong compatibility. Why, she practically heard wedding bells whenever he walked by, a phenomenon she did not understand or like one bit.

Fate?

Nah, she told herself. More likely that imp, Cupid, up to his old tricks again. She'd proved herself an easy mark for this kind of guy, after all, and more than once...but that was years ago. These days, she had her head on straight, knew what—or who—was needed to make her happy. And her scoring of Tyler as a possible mate just meant she was ready to find that happiness. She would undoubtedly rate every single man she met in just the same way. It was something that single women on the downhill slide to thirty naturally did.

Chapter Five

After dinner, everyone congregated in the den for the evening news. When that was over, Tyler announced he was making a run to a nearby discount store for some essentials and asked if anyone else wanted to go.

John, at that moment banging on their aged television to clear the picture, made the immediate decision to buy a new one. Since avid television addicts Carly and Tim naturally begged to help him pick it out, Julie volunteered to keep Josh and soon found herself alone with her nephew in a house blessedly quiet.

She headed upstairs immediately, where she set Josh on the floor with his favorite toys. Now was the perfect time to get herself a bath, she thought, when Tyler would not be next door listening to every splash. Josh would be okay in the childproofed room if she locked the hall door so he couldn't get out and kept her connecting bathroom door open so she could keep track of him.

Julie did just that, twisting the skeleton key in the antique lock of the door separating her bedroom from the hall then hiding it out of Josh's reach. She next shut the bathroom door that opened into Tyler's room, firmly pushing in the button to secure its more modern knob lock. Leaving the other bathroom door—the one to her room—ajar, she filled the tub with hot, bubbly water. One ear ever on her nephew, talking gibberish to his toys, she proceeded to treat herself to a long soak that was pure heaven.

"Josh...are you okay?" Julie called out several minutes later.

"Dokeydokey," came the reply, kid talk for *okey-dokey,* one of Grandpa John's favorite expressions.

Julie smiled and closed her eyes. Muscles she hadn't even realized were tense began to relax and her thoughts to wander. Consciousness soon slipped a notch, depositing her in the netherworld just before slumber. There, sounds such as testing twists of an antique doorknob, the subsequent opening of a bathroom door already ajar, the scoot of a child's step stool and even the click of a modern knob lock were heard but not interpreted as escape of a little boy far too clever for his aunt Julie.

"Just three more steps and we're there," said John, who helped Tyler lug a box full of big-screen television up the front porch steps. Carly and Tim fairly danced around Tyler in their excitement over the purchase, further complicating his precarious backward ascent.

But they made it and then inched their way to the den, where the set was deposited on the floor opposite the couch, recliner and love seat.

"Let's get this baby hooked up, shall we?" John said to his grandchildren, already ripping into the box.

Tyler moved to help, only to stop when he spied Josh tossing building blocks made of some kind of spongy material down the stairs. Puzzled to see the child unsupervised, Tyler left the den without a word and without being noticed by John and his busy grandkids.

He jogged up the stairs, scooped up the tyke, then headed to Julie's room to find out what had happened to her. Normally she watched the little boy like a hawk....

He found her door closed and locked. Baffled and more than a little concerned, Tyler turned on his heel, toddler still in tow, and walked to his own sleeping quarters, intending to enter Julie's room via the shared bathroom.

"Dada," Josh sang out just as Tyler burst into the bathroom.

At once water sloshed in the tub. A glance in that direction revealed Julie, neck-deep in a sea of bubbles. She screamed. Tyler yelped. Josh began to cry.

Tyler instantly backed out of the bathroom and sat on his bed, face flushed, heart thumping. He tried to soothe Josh, who he'd apparently scared half to death, not an easy task since his mind wasn't on that but on Julie, now scrambling out of the tub if the splashes, drips and soft curses he heard were anything to judge by.

Not two seconds later she stormed into the room, covered from head to toe by a thick terry cloth robe. "Just what do you think you're doing?"

"Rescuing Josh."

"Rescuing...?" Julie froze, obviously just noticing her nephew, now sniffling instead of crying outright.

She glanced back over her shoulder at the bathroom, saw the stool and turned pale as a ghost. "Oh my God. Where was he?"

"By the stairs."

Julie pressed a hand to her chest as though having a heart attack. "Why, that little monkey! I never dreamed he could manage that door." She sucked in a deep breath. "Thanks for saving him. It's a wonder he didn't tumble right down those stairs."

"Yeah," Tyler murmured even as Josh reached out for his aunt. She shook a stern finger at him, then shook her head, grinned and stretched out her arms. Tyler handed the boy over to her without a word.

"I'm, uh, sorry I yelled at you." Julie didn't look at Tyler when she said the words, instead nuzzling the top of Josh's head.

"Forgiven. But that's not what this is really about, is it?"

"Excuse me?"

"You thought I deliberately walked in on you."

"That's ridiculous!" she retorted, but she did not meet his gaze.

Tyler sighed, unconvinced. "I know you don't want me here, Julie. I swear I'll leave as soon as I find a place—surely no more than a week, maybe two." Tyler stood and walked over to his window. Since it was dark out, he saw nothing but his own reflection in the panes, and, behind his, hers and the boy's. "Meanwhile you can rest assured that your privacy will be respected. In fact, I'll do my best to make sure you don't even know I'm around."

For a moment Julie just looked at him, her expression unreadable. "That suits me fine. Now did Dad find a television?"

Tyler nodded. "He and the other kids probably have it hooked up by now."

"Good." That said, Julie, Josh in her arms, vanished into the bathroom. Moments later Tyler heard the other connecting door shut firmly.

Though he knew he should go down to see if John needed help, Tyler instead kicked off his loafers and stretched out on Don's bed. He closed his eyes and was treated instantly to a vision of Julie as she'd looked in the tub mere minutes ago. He saw again her dark hair, twisted up in a knot at the back of her head except for a few tendrils, which had escaped and clung wetly to her slender neck. He saw her eyes, wide with shock, and her mouth, a kissable O of surprise. He also saw her skin—what wasn't hidden by sliding islands of bubbles, anyway—and noted how soft, how touchably soft her body appeared to be.

Tyler instantly wished the bubbles hadn't hidden the good parts. But it was easy to use his imagination to fill in the blanks, expanding on the accuracy of his memory until he created a Technicolor fantasy that had nothing to do with reality. In the homemade vision, Julie stepped out of the tub and into his waiting arms. He carried her to this very bed, where they lay together, exploring the hills and valleys of her physique and his.

What a dream...breathtaking...so realistic that his body readied itself for the imaginary encounter. As he had before, Tyler marveled at the intensity of his desire for Julie. She could become an obsession, he realized. In fact, she might be one already.

So what did one do to an obsession who had a dad, two brothers, a sister and various other relatives hovering too close for comfort? Well, making love to her was certainly not an option since one or more of those kin were liable to burst in at any moment unannounced. Tyler thought what a scandal that would be and was treated to another fantasy—one that involved shotguns and weddings.

No, he'd definitely have to keep his hands—and kisses—to himself. Besides . . . even if Julie were willing and the two of them could find time alone, he wouldn't be home free. Their goals were too damn different and the very scruples that sent him scurrying eight years ago were still alive and well. A man who preferred companionship on an as-needed basis had no business getting involved with a woman so obviously caught up in forever afters. Neither could win, and that was for damn sure.

Through the walls, Tyler suddenly heard voices—muffled but unmistakably those of Julie and a jabbering Josh. He then heard her laughter, magical and light.

What were they doing? he wondered, experiencing a sharp stab of what could only be loneliness. Wincing at the pain—almost physical—Tyler decided that now must be one of those needy times for him, a time when he could use a little company. Wisely, he stayed put, resisting the temptation to knock on her connecting door, join the pair at whatever they were doing and appease this intense longing to belong. Why, by the time he got in there, it might be gone.

Or maybe not. Maybe it might last an hour this time or maybe several. Hell, it might last all day. If anyone could make him that crazy, Julie could. What else could explain how she'd haunted his dreams for eight years? Why she influenced his every decision now?

Pilot for New-Ware, huh? Stunned, Tyler lay there and for the first time acknowledged just what he'd done: given up the freedom to fly when and where *he* wanted so he could fly Julie when and where *she* wanted. He had to be stark raving bonkers. Why, he'd quit a great job to be his own man. And now here he was...*hers*.

Well, maybe not exactly, he reminded himself. He would be flying Don and John some, too. But the bottom line was the same, and it could not be denied—Julie was the reason he ever considered this job. Julie was the reason he'd taken it.

So what now?

Take certain steps, that's what. First of all, he'd call up Ronnie Kimsey and commit himself to a few air shows come summer. That would ensure retention of Tyler's identity. Second, he'd watch—watch for impending danger by second-guessing every move he made, every move she made, every move anyone made. Heck, he'd even keep an eye on this old house. Big enough for one more, built solidly of love, the dwelling made him think of, and then long for, things he didn't really want: home-cooked meals, family ties, babies.

Tyler shuddered, then grinned at his own reaction. Obviously he wasn't lost yet. If he took those steps and if he stole a moment right now to renew his vows of bachelorhood, freedom and adventure, he'd probably be safe until he got out of this place.

Somberly, deliberately, Tyler stole the moment.

The sound of running water woke Julie on Monday morning. Try as she might, she could not go back to sleep so lay beside the still-slumbering Josh and listened to the sounds of Tyler's toilette in the bathroom next door.

She could follow his every move, thanks to the thin walls, and so knew exactly when he stepped from the tub. Imagination—and leftover marriage memories—took control then, providing her with a picture of Tyler toweling himself dry, wrapping the clinging towel to his middle, combing his hair and shaving. Julie recalled how she used to sit on the side of the bathtub to watch Cord shave.

She realized she missed doing that. Realized she missed Cord.

Or did she? Admittedly, marriage to Cord had not always been good or even pleasant, though she'd loved him like crazy. Almost from the start, they'd been at each other's throats, arguing over things that did not matter, avoiding issues that did.

It was a clear case of mismatch, and for years bitterness had colored her memories. Today, however, all she could really recall were the happy moments. Were the sad times, then, forgotten? It seemed so, and Julie smiled. Stretching lazily, she experienced a sense of wellness that started in her toes and worked its way clear up to the top of her head until she felt incredibly energized, gloriously free.

Sitting abruptly upright, Julie leaned forward and stretched again, this time reaching for those tingling toes. God, but it was good to be alive. And the best part was that the whole rest of her life waited—a book of pages that had no writing on them.

Young, passionate, fertile, she could pick and choose how to fill each page. Julie vowed to do it without ink blots or misspelled words. No cross outs, no scratch throughs this time. Not even one. She'd write her life with care, with caution, keeping in mind longtime goals too long ignored.

She'd put herself back in circulation, using her head instead of her heart when picking out her next Mr. Wonderful. Life would be lived as it was meant to be. Closing her eyes, drawing in a deep, cleansing breath, Julie solemnly promised herself that.

"Are you okay?"

The question came from John, who gave Julie a funny look across the breakfast table.

"I'm just perfect. And you?" The words came out in a perky lilt.

"Uh...fine." He didn't look too sure of that, or maybe he doubted *her* answer.

Julie ignored him as she ignored all the others at the table, Kit and Tyler included. So what if their frowns said they noted a change in her? They might as well get used to the new Julie McCrae. She was there to stay...and not a moment too soon.

Right after breakfast John and Tyler left for the New-Ware factory. Though Julie knew they would visit the airport after that, she didn't let any blue mood steal her newfound contentment. She had better things to do, namely drive that gorgeous red Corvette—a refreshing change from her dad's company car—to the New-Ware office where she worked, writing advertisement copy and scheduling demonstrations when not on the road.

Leaving the kids to the care of a trusted senior citizen who sometimes helped out—Kit had to work today, too—Julie drove to the factory and stayed until after five without seeing her dad or Tyler. She spoke on the phone with Don in Montana, who demanded to know if Tyler had won his race. With a huff of impatience, Julie informed Don that he had not.

When Julie returned to the Newman house, she found Josh, Tim and Carly watching Barney on the new television. Their gazes were glued to the set, as was the gaze of the only adult in the room—Tyler. Stretched out on the floor next to Josh, the pilot wore form-fitting jeans, sweatshirt and had bare feet. Julie noted that he'd wadded a pillow and stuffed it behind his head. Josh, however, used Tyler's biceps as a prop.

Lordy, what a sight...especially to a woman whose biological clock ticked double-time. With a gulp she slipped soundlessly through the room and fairly flew up the stairs to the safety of her bedroom, where she shimmied out of her slip and panty hose—inventions of a sadistic male, she felt sure—and pulled on sweatpants and an oversize sweatshirt. Fluffy bunny house slippers completed her at-home ensemble, and grinning at the picture she made, Julie headed downstairs to the kitchen.

Since it was Monday night—a busy one for the Newmans—Julie prepared hot dogs, which were easy to serve in shifts, if necessary. John, who'd been hiding in his home office, ate first and then left for his regularly scheduled league bowling game. Kit, Carly and Tim grabbed their hot dogs on the way out the door to a birthday party for which they were late, thanks to Kit's having to work overtime. That left only Tyler, Josh and Julie to dine at leisure, which they finally did around six-thirty.

Tyler brought Josh into the kitchen the moment Julie called out that the food was ready. They sat at the bar, the three of them, Josh between the adults so he wouldn't fall out of the stool he insisted upon sitting on. As Tyler ate his chili dog, he imagined the picture they might make to anyone peeking in through the window.

Surely that of the ideal family, complete with a dad, a mom and a cute kid.

What a joke, he thought somewhat grimly, nonetheless trying on the role for size. It felt different, weird, but not really that bad.

Splat!

Tyler started violently, then scraped baked beans, just thrown by Josh, off his five-o'clock-shadowed chin.

"Joshua Michael Newman!" Julie scolded, hopping off her stool to retrieve a paper towel. Obviously appalled by her nephew's table manners, she dampened the towel then handed it to Tyler, who cleaned off the rest of the sticky mess. "We're very sorry... aren't we Josh?"

"Dokeydokey," her nephew agreed, grabbing up another handful of beans.

"Oh, no you don't," Julie scolded as she stole the child's ammo and then his plate. "I'll just take this, young man, since you're obviously not as hungry as I thought."

Josh's bottom lip began to quiver, his huge eyes to swim in tears.

Heaven help us, Tyler thought, rudely reminded that the sea of life seldom provided smooth sailing. So much for fatherhood fantasies, and thanks to the powers that be for the wake-up pinch.

With a heavy sigh Julie handed Josh a hot dog bun, which he squashed in one hand and began to mutilate with his few teeth. It was pretty gross to watch, really, even for a pilot with a strong stomach.

So as soon as was polite, Tyler escaped to his room where he lay on his bed and listened to a portable radio that must be Don's. He refused to think further about Julie, about Josh, about anything even remotely related to all that family and commitment stuff. Insanity, all such thoughts...especially for a man who loved nothing better than flying loop-de-loops over a deserted canyon somewhere just for the thrill of it. Daddies and husbands didn't do that sort of thing if they were the least bit responsible.

And just the thought of sacrificing such fun made him feel stifled and a little panicked, further reinforcing his belief that he'd never be ready to settle down. Tyler came by his revulsion honestly, he believed. Prior experience with another large family had left a very bitter taste in his mouth. And though he knew all such families weren't the same, he still felt awkward and wary around them. How else could a siblingless son of a single mom feel? Why, his own dad, an investigative journalist, had chosen freedom over the ties of marriage and fatherhood.

So why did Tyler keep agonizing over the issue like he had some big decision to make? He didn't have a clue and was afraid to wonder.

He might not like the answer he found.

Tuesday started out much the same as Monday, but by night the house had lost some of its usual occupants. Kit, suddenly finding herself with a few days off, hopped in her car and headed to Seattle, home of her in-laws. Carly and Tim left with their real dad's parents, who stopped by to get them en route to Boise for an after-Christmas get-together with their son. All would return on Sunday.

For that reason the house was eerily quiet when Julie got home from work. She did not waver from her usual routine of changing clothes, then heading to the kitchen, so was quite surprised to find Tyler already there and setting his famous pot roast on the table.

"Voilà!" he said and grinned.

Julie had to grin back at the sight he made wearing his usual jeans and shirt, plus one of her ruffle-trimmed bib aprons and a baseball cap, turned bill backward.

When he realized her gaze was on the cap, he shrugged. "You don't have one of those white caps like chefs wear... at least I didn't find one."

"No," she agreed. "But I do have an apron more suitable." Reaching into the pantry, she extracted the white canvas bib apron her father wore when barbecuing.

Tyler wasted no time taking off the calico apron and substituting John's.

"It smells delicious," Julie said, sniffing the aromatic steam rising from the roast and vegetables surrounding it.

"Thanks." Tyler walked to the door that connected to the den and whistled. "Come and get it!"

John and Josh did.

Moments later, the four of them sat at the table, eating what proved to be an excellent meal. She noted that Tyler seemed much more relaxed than usual and wondered why. Could it be that the size of the Newman clan overwhelmed him sometimes? Julie had seen that happen before and even felt it herself. In time most people adjusted. Would Tyler adjust, too? Somehow she doubted it... and didn't care, anyway. Her family was everything to her. Everything.

Since Julie volunteered for clean-up, the men headed to the den to watch television, where they stayed until bedtime. Julie retreated to her room long before then. Tyler, so at ease tonight, really felt like family. She didn't care for that unsettling sensation. He wasn't family and never would be.

An incident Wednesday night proved even more disconcerting. After another family-type dinner, this one prepared by Julie, everyone moved to the den to watch a documentary on whales. John, realizing he'd seen it before, soon abandoned them for his office. Josh left, too, toddling after John, but was soon back and bothering Tyler, who, though patient, obviously wanted to see the film.

With a huff of exasperation for little boys who sure could be pests, Julie got up from the recliner to do what any good aunt would do—rescue Tyler from the child crawling all over him. Stepping to the couch, where Tyler patiently wrestled Josh, she reached out for her nephew, who clung to their guest's neck for dear life, his little feet firmly planted between the cushions of the couch, next to Tyler's right thigh.

"Come on, sweetie," she urged from Tyler's left side as she worked to free Josh's choke hold on him. Josh resisted Julie's efforts, then, squealing impishly, threw both arms around her neck and fell back flat on the cushion, an action that caught her off guard and took her down with him.

Now sprawled over Tyler, Julie struggled to regain her feet without squashing Josh, an impossible task thanks to the fact that Tyler suddenly wrapped his arms around her.

Josh laughed like crazy, highly entertained by their antics, then rolled out from under Julie and scrambled off the couch, headed toward the back of the house yelling "Gamps! Gamps!" at the top of his lungs.

"Come back here!" Julie called after him as she struggled to get up, the next instant glaring over her shoulder at Tyler and snapping, "Would you please let go?"

"It's going to cost you," he answered, a reply that made her freeze in position.

And what a position it was—perfect for a spanking. Mortified, disconcertingly turned on, Julie abruptly renewed her attempts to escape and finally managed to turn so that her backside rested on his muscled thighs.

Heavens, but he smelled good. Her heart began to thump. Her gaze locked with his, mere inches away, then dropped to his mouth.

"And just what is the price of freedom?" she asked, dead certain she played with fire, helpless to stop.

"A kiss," he answered without hesitation.

"But Dad and Josh—"

"Aren't in here," Tyler finished for her, words Julie's quick glance over his shoulder revealed were true. "Kiss me, Julie."

"No."

"Kiss me."

How could she resist, when his eyes glowed with curiosity that surely mirrored her own and told her he, too, wondered how much time had changed things? Telling herself that same curiosity was the only reason she would ever experiment in this way, Julie abruptly pressed her mouth to Tyler's.

Chapter Six

Tyler grunted his satisfaction with her decision, then tightened his embrace. His tongue immediately teased to deepen the kiss. Julie cooperated without hesitation, savoring the taste so distinctly Tyler, a taste sweet enough to haunt her the past eight years. When he broke the contact a moment later, it was to trail kisses over her cheeks, chin, earlobe and then neck.

So nothing had changed...nothing. He still drove her wild. Probably always would.

Giving in to the moment, Julie dipped her head back to give him better access. She panted for breath—as always short of it when he was around—then shivered when he pressed his lips to a particularly sensitive spot that sent goose bumps dancing up her arms. It didn't help that he moved his hands in time to the kisses, smooth strokes on her arms, her back, her bare breasts.

Her bare breasts? Damn. Half-drunk on Tyler's kisses, wishing she hadn't ditched her bra with her slip and panty hose earlier that night, Julie struggled for the will to push his hands away.

"You've got to stop," she whispered urgently, finally slapping at his skillful fingers, tugging down her shirt.

"Why?" Tyler asked, and for the life of her, Julie couldn't think of a single good reason.

That was just as well. Wrapping his arms around Julie again, Tyler once more covered her mouth with his, making any sort of reply impossible. Julie tensed, but just for a moment before giving in to crazy desire and kissing him back.

He tugged her bottom lip with his teeth, then thrust his tongue deep inside her mouth again and again. It was a primitive motion—a sensual reminder of the basic movement of love. Julie began to sweat, hot for him. So hot for him.

Her thoughts flew to her room. She pictured her bed and instantly wondered what Josh would say if she kicked him out of it for the night so Tyler could share her pillow.

Would the toddler throw a fit?

More important, would dear old Dad?

As if in reply, a soft "Ahem!" was heard, coming from the direction of the door.

"Dad!" Julie exclaimed, so desperate to extricate herself from Tyler that she fell off his lap and onto the carpet with a soft "Ouch!"

John, holding Josh in his arms, did not react beyond a telltale twitch of his bottom lip and a twinkle in his eye. "I'm taking Josh upstairs to get his bath. Then I'm putting him to bed. That should take me an hour, at least."

"So?" Julie demanded as she scrambled to her feet and self-consciously smoothed down her shirt.

"So I won't be down again for at least that long and maybe not then." He faked a yawn. "I'm really tired..."

"Just what are you telling me?" Julie asked, though she knew damn well.

"I'm telling you to proceed," he replied, then turned on his heel and left without so much as a backward glance.

"Well, hell," Julie muttered, shifting her gaze from the empty door to Tyler.

For a full second they just looked at each other. Then he burst into laughter, great gulps of mirth that showed no signs of abating in the near future. While Julie glared, Tyler fell over on the couch, clutching his belly as if his giant guffaws might do him bodily harm.

Ready to harm him, herself, Julie spun around and stalked straight through the kitchen and out the back door onto the deck. There she leaned against the rail and let the freezing winter air work its magic on her flaming cheeks.

Predictably, Tyler followed some moments later, walking over to join her at the rail.

"You okay?"

"Okay? How could I possibly be okay? I feel like a teenager caught slipping in after curfew, dammit, and I'm twenty-five years old!"

"Which is certainly old enough for a little kissing in the den," Tyler reminded her.

"Just kissing...?" Had he forgotten she let him go beyond that...heaven help her?

"That was all your dad saw. At least I think so. And so what if it wasn't? I mean, he did tell us to proceed, didn't he?"

"That's not the point!" Julie edged away from Tyler. God, but men were idiots.

"Then what is?" he demanded, closing the gap between them.

"The point is I had no business being in that position in the first place."

When Julie would've moved away again, Tyler caught her by the shoulders, preventing it. "Why not? You're legal and free, as am I."

"All the more reason for us to be careful." Impatiently she shook off his touch and walked clear to the end of the deck, the exact spot where they'd first kissed eight years ago. She didn't think about that until Tyler followed, then old memories returned, forceful as a punch to the gut.

He looked exactly as he had back then—great body, dashing good looks, eyes that glowed with unmistakable desire. What woman could resist such a man? Certainly not Julie, who sagged against the rail, heart thumping wildly.

"Could you just speak English? All I'm asking is what's so bad about our fooling around in your dad's den."

"I'll tell you what's so bad," Julie answered, suddenly furious with herself. "How you make me feel, that's what. It isn't right. It isn't good. It isn't even—"

Tyler's lips smothered the rest of her sentence, which was quickly forgotten in the wake of one devastating kiss. Clearly, she had no willpower where he was concerned.

Clearly, he knew it.

Head spinning, Julie wedged her hands between their plastered bodies and somehow pushed him away.

"Now what's wrong?" he asked, without a doubt baffled.

"The same thing that was wrong before you kissed me!" She turned her back to him and looked out over the yard, glowing silver in the moonlight. The sight of all that snow reminded Julie that she didn't have on a coat and so she should be freezing. Fat chance! Tyler's body radiated heat better than any fireplace...or did that warm glow come from deep inside her own?

"If it's any consolation," he said, his voice soft against the back of her head, "you make me crazy, too."

"Consolation, my foot! That just makes things worse." Julie heaved a sigh of impatience, then turned around to face him. "Don't you see the danger? We're mismatches, Tyler. Oh, our physical needs might be equal, all right, but emotionally we're worlds apart and always will be."

"I assume you're referring to your search for the perfect husband."

"Not perfect. *Normal.*"

"Normal as in...?"

"A man with a nine-to-five job that offers good benefits and the weekends free. A man who wants a house and children, PTA, little league, vacations to Disneyland."

"Pilots may not always work those particular hours, Julie, but as a rule, they're just as normal as the next man." Trust him to hone in on the characteristic that mattered least, ignoring the important ones.

"Some, maybe," Julie had to agree. "Not you, though. Why, I'll bet you're still planning to fly with the air show next summer, aren't you?"

Tyler winced. "I, uh, haven't made up my mind yet."

"Sure you haven't."

"I haven't!"

"So what are you going to do instead...climb a cliff, dive for buried treasure in shark-infested waters, hang glide?"

"I have never hang glided."

"Oh? Well, you're slipping, Tyler Jordan. But what do I care? The issue, here, is not your death wish or unsuitability as a husband. It's the fact that if I satisfy my desire for a man by 'fooling around' with the likes of you, then I won't be as eager as I should to find the man of my dreams. More important, there's that one-in-a-million chance we might actually fall in love, God forbid, and if that happened, I'd never get what I want." She looked Tyler dead in the eye. "Does this make any sense at all?"

"Yeah. Yeah it does."

They exchanged a long look, neither speaking. Then Tyler brushed her cheek with his hand, cleared his throat and said, "I'll, um, see you tomorrow morning, I guess. We're still leaving at nine?"

"Nine?" It took her a second to recall that Tyler would be flying her to Yakima, Washington, for a cookware demonstration tomorrow. *Damn.*

"Oh, yeah, sure." She faked a smile. "I, um, hope what happened tonight won't compromise our working relationship."

"I've been a professional pilot for years, Julie. I can fly with *anyone.*" He said it as though she were some undesirable he'd been hired to cart around. "Good night," he added and then left.

Julie shivered and, suddenly cold, hurried indoors herself.

She looks nervous.

Standing by the Bonanza the next morning, Tyler watched as Julie approached him, a slight frown knitting her brow. When her gaze swept the plane from nose to tail, he remembered that she'd never seen it before. Judging from her worried expression, he guessed she'd probably not seen many others this size, either, and certainly not flown in one.

Tyler opened the door of the aircraft, stepped onto the wing, then lowered his body through the opening into the passenger seat.

"Slip off your heels and step right here," he told Julie, pointing to a reinforced area on the top of the wing near the door of the red, white and blue aircraft. Soft-soled shoes were fine. The high heels she wore were not.

Julie slipped off her pumps and tried to do as requested, but couldn't make the giant step until she handed Tyler her shoes and hiked up the straight skirt of her navy blue suit. Then, grasping the hand he extended to her and the handhold on the side of the plane, she stepped onto the wing. Tyler, who scooted over into the pilot's seat, caught a glimpse of stockinged thigh and then lacy panties as she stepped aboard and sort of fell into the seat. Visibly flustered, she jerked down the skirt and slipped back into her shoes.

Since all her paraphernalia had been loaded into the luggage space earlier and they were now ready for take-off, Tyler demonstrated how Julie should scoot her seat up under the yolk. He next started the engine and reached across her to close the door.

Donning the radio headset that was his contact with the tower, Tyler began a preflight ritual that included taxiing down the runway, a run up to see that everything worked properly and then takeoff. He made a special effort to set Julie at ease during the one-hour flight that followed, beginning with a recitation of some positive safety statistics. He was rewarded by the obvious lessening of her tension. By the time they landed in Yakima, she actually laughed and talked, gesturing with hands that had once held the seat in a white-knuckled clutch.

After deboarding, Julie headed straight into the terminal to rent a car, leaving Tyler to unload her demonstration supplies outside. By the time he rolled her collapsible luggage cart, now loaded down, into the terminal, she was finished at the counter. Together they walked to the station wagon she had rented.

Stashing everything in back took several minutes, after which Tyler slipped behind the steering wheel and drove to the department store in one of the malls, a store he knew well since it was near his apartment. There, he once again unloaded her gear and rolled it inside the store.

"Thanks," she told him after they made their presence known to the manager, then made their way to the part of the store that featured housewares.

Tyler reached for the folding table strapped to the luggage carrier. "So how long do these demonstrations last?" he asked as he set it up.

"About an hour and a half." Julie spread a cloth over the table. "If it takes longer to get your apartment cleaned out, that's okay. I'll just wander over to ladies' wear and scope out the latest fashions until you come back for me."

"Actually, I was thinking I'd just hang around here until you were finished. Then you can go with me to the apartment. I have several hours worth of packing up to do, and four hands are better than two, you know."

"You mean you're going to stay here and watch my demonstration?"

"Yes. Unless it'll distract you."

Julie positively glared at him. "I've done this demonstration dozens of times, Tyler. Nothing and *no one* makes me nervous."

"Good. So, what can I do to help?"

"Unpack that box," she replied and then turned her back on him.

Tyler did as requested, keeping one eye on Julie, who skillfully arranged her merchandise. A reminder announcement over the loudspeaker resulted in the gradual gathering of a crowd of shoppers, and twenty minutes later Julie held up a cookbook and began her talk.

Tyler drifted to the back of the crowd and watched Julie with a critical eye. Would every man find her as tempting as this poor ol' pilot? he asked himself. Beginning at the twist of hair on top of her head, he made a slow, if not impartial, inspection, letting his gaze linger on each part of her body as he pondered the question.

He noted first her face, beautiful by any man's standards. Next came the curve of her neck—an area his lips had traced on more than one occasion. The flesh there smelled particularly nice, he remembered, smiling to himself and moving on.

With every gesture Julie's unbuttoned jacket shifted, revealing a white crepe blouse so thin he could see the lace of her slip. Did she wear a bra today? he wondered, remembering last night's surprise of bare breasts. Man, oh man, but he wanted to touch them again. Gulping, Tyler dragged his gaze lower.

Julie had a tiny waist. Oh, not necessarily Scarlett O'Hara tiny, but certainly small enough to make a man feel big in comparison. Tyler liked that. He also liked the curve of her hips, the length of her legs, the— Hell, he liked every millimeter of her body, even the areas as yet unexplored by his hands, lips or... whatever.

Yeah, she was a woman any man would be proud to claim, and acknowledging that, Tyler looked around, suddenly fearful her Mr. Right would stroll up and snatch her away. Housewares would be a good place for a nerd like that to hang out. Restless now, impatient to take her away, Tyler tuned back in to what Julie was saying.

"...free cookbook with every purchase of our deluxe set, now on sale today..."

Tyler tuned her back out, but still stared, now noting her rapport with the crowd, most of whom were women, thank goodness. He thought that if he were one of those onlookers, he'd be jealous of Julie, but these ladies just smiled and nodded at her. Tyler suspected that some sets of the cookware would be sold, a fact proved true when several customers headed to the store display the moment Julie finished up her demonstration.

As soon as the crowd thinned, Tyler made his way to where Julie stood at the table, handing out business cards and colorful brochures to anyone who wanted them. He waited until every last person had deserted them, then gave her a thumbs-up that made her smile.

"So how'd I do?"

"Great. Perfect." *Just don't give me a pop quiz.*

"I'd kill for a cold drink," she said, tilting her head to one side, eyes pleading.

"Then why don't you go get one while I pack up? Better yet, get us some lunch somewhere, why don't you?" He reached for his billfold, only to halt when she shook her head.

"It's on Dad," she told him with a light laugh.

In a second Tyler stood alone. Grinning, he began the work of reloading all Julie's boxes and securing them to the luggage cart again. Just as he finished, she returned, two soft drinks and a paper sack in hand.

"Here," she said, offering him one of the drinks.

Tyler took it gratefully and sipped it as they walked out to the station wagon. Once behind the wheel and headed to his apartment, he glanced over at Julie, now staring out the window. She still sipped, and every time her ruby lips pursed around the end of the candy-striped straw, Tyler's heart thumped extra hard.

Damn, but the woman got to him.

Just not enough to sacrifice his freedom for her dreams.

Cute, Julie thought, eyeing first Tyler, who looked good enough to kidnap today, then the outside of his garage apartment, mere minutes from the mall. Refusing his offer to let her go first, she followed him up steep stairs to a tiny porch of sorts, where he dug out his key and then opened the door.

The place smelled a bit musty, not unusual in an apartment minus its occupant for several weeks. A damp chill permeated the air. Tyler quickly turned on the gas heater, which soon raised the temperature in the one-room apartment several degrees.

Meanwhile they sat at his tiny wooden table and shivered while they ate the hamburgers and fries Julie had purchased at the mall. Neither talked while they ate, so the sounds she heard were the hiss of the heater, the rattle of ice in paper cups, the crackle of food wrappers, wadded and tossed into the trash bag.

"So where do you want to start?" she asked, getting up from the table.

"First on my agenda is telling my landlord I'm leaving," Tyler replied with a glance out the window toward the house next door. "First on yours should be changing clothes. I'm not much of a housekeeper, so the dust is gonna fly when we start throwing things in boxes." All at once his shoulders sagged. "Boxes...! I don't have any boxes."

"Didn't I see a convenience store down the block?"

"Yeah."

"Why don't I go see if they have any?"

"I have a better idea," Tyler replied with a hopeful grin. "Why don't you go tell my landlord I'm leaving, and *I'll* go get the boxes."

Julie just laughed, snatched up the car key, and headed back out the door.

As it turned out, she was only able to get four boxes at the store on the corner. They directed her to another one, just a few blocks away, and there she hit the jackpot, returning to the apartment some thirty minutes later with more than enough boxes jammed into the rented car.

Back inside the apartment she found Tyler busy pulling clothes out of his closet and tossing them in a heap on the floor. She noticed he'd changed clothes and taken off his shoes.

"So how'd it go?" she asked as she slipped out of her coat.

"Let's just say he was less than thrilled by all the notice he's getting. My deposit was even in jeopardy for a minute or two, but I promised to leave the place spick-and-span."

"Hmm. Well, we'd better get started, hadn't we?"

"Not until you put these on." Tyler handed her a pair of sweats and socks and a white T-shirt, no doubt his. Eyeing the clothes, which would certainly be too large, Julie headed to the bathroom to change out of her good things. Minutes later she emerged in her borrowed garb. Tyler, who now wore tattered blue jeans and a Seattle Seahawks T-shirt, whistled his appreciation, then ducked when she threw the first thing she could find, luckily a sofa pillow.

They worked quickly, filling up the boxes that Tyler retrieved from the car. Julie noted that the shelf-lined walls, when bereft of the dozens of trophies, plaques and ribbons stashed there, seemed to close in on them, lending an intimacy to the experience of turning Tyler's home into a house.

When he moved to strip the bed, she hesitated before pitching in to help, almost reluctant to participate even though the width of the mattress separated them.

"Man, I hate doing this," Tyler grumbled. "I just changed these sheets before I left—something I put off way too long since I don't have a washing machine—and I haven't even slept on them."

"Well, we don't have time for a nap," Julie told him as she tugged back the blankets.

"True, but there are things we can do—things that won't take nearly as long as a nap."

"No, Tyler," Julie said—at least that's what she *tried* to say. Unfortunately the words came out *Oh, Tyler,* and sounded as wistful as she felt. So what was the harm in a teeny-tiny fling with such a delectable Mr. Wrong? she instantly wondered, eyeing him from head to toe. Why, a girl had to do *something* while waiting for her Mr. Right to show up.

Tyler's look of surprise told Julie he heard the words just the way they were said. While she summoned the will to clarify the mistake, he rounded the end of the bed, and catching her up in a bear hug, fell sideways on the crisp, clean sheets.

"Tyler! I—" she began, breathy words his hungry kisses obliterated. At once Julie's good sense flew right out the nearby window, abandoning her to emotion and sensation.

And what sensations...a whole barrage of them, ranging from shivers of delight to tingles of anticipation. Tyler's hands seemed to be everywhere at once, and when Julie realized she'd somehow lost her T-shirt, she simply sighed, sat up and coaxed him out of his.

Tyler grunted his enthusiasm for her cooperation, then he lay her back against the pillows again so he could unclasp her bra and caress her bare breasts. Julie treasured the heat of his touch—marveled at the warmth now spreading from his hands throughout her body.

She moved her own hands over his bare back, smooth muscled to her touch and evidence of his considerable strength. Though Julie would've loved to rush their encounter to the ultimate fulfillment, Tyler took his time. Maddeningly, gloriously he tasted each breast in turn, teasing the tips to pebble hardness before trailing his mouth down her midriff.

Julie caught her breath and, suddenly unable to lie still, raised herself up and pushed Tyler flat on his back. Since she caught him off guard, it was easy. Propping her elbow on the bed next to his pillow, resting her head on her hand, she curled her body close and traced lazy circles on his chest with her fingertips.

He sighed his delight with her teasing touch and, reaching up, pulled her down so he could kiss her.

"I want you. I always have," he whispered, soft words that shimmied down her spine. With an answering sigh Julie shifted her body so that her breasts crushed against his chest. To her surprise Tyler wrapped his arms around her and rolled clean over, a move that put her partially under him, her back pressed into the sheets once more.

His gaze locked with hers, he palmed one breast, then slid his flattened hand down her midriff. He moved in slow motion, almost as if he waited for her to yell Stop! but Julie said nothing. Just as deliberately, Tyler slipped his hand beneath the waistband of her borrowed sweatpants. Julie tensed when his fingers encountered the bare flesh of her belly and the elastic top of her bikini panties. Tyler instantly ceased all exploration, clearly waiting for her permission to proceed. With a wiggle of impatience, Julie gave him the go ahead, and his fingers dipped under the elastic.

"Tyler! Tyler Jordan! Are you in there?"

At the sound of the booming male voice, they both started so violently that the headboard of the bed slammed into the wall.

"Ignore him," Tyler whispered.

It wasn't easy.

"Tyler, where are you?" demanded the voice again even as the doorknob rattled. They heard a soft curse, then the jangle of keys.

Spitting out a curse of his own—one that made Julie wince—Tyler yanked his hand free of her clothes and sprang off the bed. In a flash he'd pulled on his T-shirt, but not before Julie snatched up her discarded clothing and darted into the bathroom. There she stood, heart racing, and listened to the landlord's news that he'd already found another renter. Resentment at his untimely intrusion welled up inside her…until she caught sight of her reflection in the mirror over the sink.

Julie could only stare in disbelief at her disheveled hair, flushed cheeks and whisker-chafed breasts. At once reality hit, and she sank to the bath mat on the floor. She sat there, stunned, until Tyler knocked on the door an eternity later.

"Julie?"

She raised her head and stared at the door with trepidation, wondering if one look at him would turn her to putty again.

"Julie, he's gone."

And so, it seems, am I, she silently replied as she got to her feet. Julie slipped on her bra, pulled the T-shirt over her head, licked her dry lips and finger combed her hair. A moment later she opened the door to find Tyler standing just outside it, obviously concerned.

"Are you all right?"

"Fine."

He eyed her for a moment, not missing a thing. "You don't look fine."

"Well, I am." Brushing past him, she stepped over to the bed and grabbed a handful of sheet and blanket, which she peeled off the bed and tossed to the floor with a vengeance. Tyler hesitated only a second before moving to the other side to help. Silently they stripped the mattress of its coverings, and it was only when the bed was bare that Julie raised her eyes to Tyler's again.

"Feel better now?" he asked, his gaze sharp and too perceptive.

She nodded.

"Just for the record...how far would you have let me go?"

She swallowed hard before giving him a mirthless laugh. "All... the way."

He let those shocking words digest. "Does this mean you've given up on finding a normal guy?"

"It does *not.* It just means I'm human, with human desires, and until I find the man of my dreams to keep me satisfied, you'll have to do."

Tyler flinched as if he'd been struck, a reaction that told Julie she'd hurt him, something she'd never intended to do. Or had she? Wasn't hurting him a way to ensure that he'd keep his distance from now on? And if he did, wouldn't she be safe from passion she could not deny, but had no business feeling?

They finished packing up in stormy silence, emptying the bureau, the kitchen cabinets and a bookcase. Though Tyler should have been thrilled that Julie would even consider an affair—all he wanted from any woman—he fumed that she expected so little of him. This unexpected reaction both baffled and disconcerted Tyler, who began to wonder if he'd slept through his watch and let a change of heart slip up on him.

Since work obviated the need for conversation, they kept at it nonstop for two solid hours—vacuuming the carpet and dusting the furniture, scouring the toilet, tubs and sinks. When not another thing could be done, Tyler declared the apartment cleaner than when he'd rented it, a sentiment with which his landlord finally agreed. Julie and Tyler quickly changed back into their original clothes and by five o'clock, they entered the terminal at the airport.

While Tyler loaded the Bonanza with all his worldly goods, Julie sat in a waiting room and watched television. Her mind wandered until a weather update flashed across the screen. Frowning, Julie read about a winter storm front headed for Idaho. Moments later a weatherman stood in front of a map that showed clearly all areas that might get heavy snowfall. To Julie's eye, a good portion of Washington and northern Idaho, location of Clear Falls, were included.

At once, old fears slammed home. She panicked, nearly knocking Tyler over when he came into the terminal to get her.

"Ready?" he asked, clearly baffled by her death clench on his arm.

Julie shook her head. "We can't go."

"What?"

"There's a weather warning. Look." Julie as good as dragged Tyler to a chair near the television.

He sat and listened to the tail end of the report, then turned his attention to Julie, seated next to him and clutching his biceps like the scaredy-cat she was. "That doesn't affect us."

"But of course it does," she argued.

"It doesn't. We'll be behind that front most of the way home and above the snow clouds when we're not."

"But—"

"But nothing. We'll be fine." For a moment he studied her face as if weighing the extent of her concern. "Of course, if you're really worried, we could spend the night here in Yakima. My rent is paid up until the end of the month, after all, so there's not much my landlord could say. We'll share the bed."

She released him then. "Not funny."

He shrugged. "Okay. We'll find a motel. Or better yet, we could just stretch out here in the waiting room."

"Don't make fun of me," Julie snapped, getting abruptly to her feet.

"Ah, honey, I'm not. Well, not much, anyway." He frowned up at her. "Are you really, truly frightened? Or just nervous?"

She considered that for a moment, then sighed. "Just nervous. I was this morning, too."

"You're kidding!" Tyler drawled. "I never even suspected. Why, you looked so cool, so calm." He grimaced, hooked each foot around a chair leg and, shaking like a leaf, grasped the armrests so tightly that his knuckles turned pale.

Julie had to laugh and felt better for it. "Was I that bad?"

"Worse... at first. But by the time we landed, you were fine, weren't you?"

"Well..."

"Come on now, admit it. Before I landed that plane here in Yakima, you were actually enjoying the flight, weren't you?"

"Maybe just a little."

He stood up to frame her face in his hands. "Then trust me again. I'm a damned good pilot, Julie, with years of experience. I'll get you to Idaho tonight."

"Promise?" she asked, unwitting echo of another time when she wondered if she could believe in him.

"I promise," he told her, and in spite of herself, she trusted him . . . just as she had before.

Chapter Seven

Even obscured by snowfall, the mountains of Washington were a sight to see. Julie couldn't relax enough to enjoy them, however, caught up in worries of takeoff and then flight.

Too soon thick clouds wrapped around the plane and obscured her view. Not soon enough the clouds became a carpet below, and clear skies stretched to forever all around. Ahead lay the navy blue of nightfall, complete with stars and a full moon. Behind shone the brilliance of sunset. Julie exhaled sharply in relief at the glorious sight and glanced over to Tyler, who flew the plane as if by instinct and with a half smile on his face. Clearly she'd overreacted earlier. Why, she didn't know. Julie was no coward... at least as a rule. Today, however, she could only be called the world's biggest wimp.

Must have something to do with the emotional roller coaster I've been on lately, she reassured herself, and immediately felt better. Of course she was rattled and a bit off balance. Lying half-naked with a man sometimes did that to a girl.

A girl? No, a woman of twenty-five, who damn well knew better.

"How are we doing?"

"*I'm* doing fine," Julie snapped, more irritated with herself for her actions that day than with Tyler for sounding like a bad nurse. "Can't speak for you."

The plane bobbed a little just then, and Julie caught her breath.

"Air pocket," Tyler told her. "There's some turbulence this evening. Probably due to the weather front."

"You don't say?"

Julie's sarcasm was not lost on Tyler, who noted with triumph that he'd irritated her just enough that she'd forgotten, for the moment, to be nervous. Good. If he kept picking at her, she might actually enjoy the rest of the flight, something he really wanted to happen.

"I have an idea," he said. "Why don't we take the scenic route to Idaho?"

She frowned. "I thought you guys had to file a flight plan or something."

"Oh, I'm not going to change course. I'm just going to dip back below the clouds for a minute so I can show you something. Are you game?"

"And if I'm not...?"

"I won't do it, of course. But I really want you to see this, Julie. It's something else."

Obviously curious, she gave him a nod of permission. Tyler gave her a thumbs-up, then flew the plane back down into the thick carpet of snow clouds. Seconds later they dropped into sight of the mountains, valleys, fields and forests that he loved second only to the sky.

Everything looked gray and a little blurry, thanks to the winter storm front, which meant early dusk and snow flurries. All the same, it was beautiful, and Tyler flew in silence for a moment, his gaze searching the landscape.

"I see it!" he suddenly exclaimed. "Look down there, to your right."

Julie did and then gasped her surprise.

"Oh, my," she whispered, reverent words that were exactly what Tyler wanted to hear. If she hadn't been impressed, he'd have been disappointed. With a grin, he dipped even lower so she could better see the panorama below.

"That snow-covered field to our left just ahead is one of the ones I dusted last spring. The farmer who owns it lives in a big white house. There! See it?"

Julie leaned forward, searching. Tyler could tell the exact moment she saw the dwelling.

"Why it looks like something off a Christmas card!" she exclaimed with a smile of delight, eyeing the two-story, white frame house now under and a little to the right of the plane.

"Yeah," Tyler murmured, taking pleasure, as always, in the sight. He didn't know exactly what appealed to him so. It was a house much like the Newman house—built of love and bursting at the seams with too large a family. He had no use for such a place, but nonetheless cherished the owner's frequent invitations to come inside for coffee or a chaotic meal with his wife and children. The man and his wife seemed to thrive on the hustle and bustle. Tyler usually left exhausted.

"I assume this farmer is married."

"Yes."

"Kids?"

"Five."

"Oh, my," she said again, her tone giving a different meaning to the exact words she'd used before. Tyler watched her expression settle into wistfulness. For once he didn't fault her for her dreams. In fact, just now, he sympathized, probably because he remembered a time or even two when he'd topped this ridge, caught sight of the farm and wished for more than he had.

Odd... but he'd forgotten those occasional longings for roots, until now. "Would you live on a spread like this?"

"Of course I would," Julie told him without hesitation.

"But it's in the middle of nowhere."

"So? If I had a husband and kids to keep me busy, I wouldn't mind." She raised her gaze from the rapidly changing scenery below and rested it on Tyler. "All I ever wanted to be was a wife and mom. Not too ambitious a career in these days of professional equality and fast-track careers, is it? In fact, my goals probably sound pretty lame to a daredevil like you."

"It doesn't matter what I think," Tyler answered, sidestepping the question. "Everyone has the right to do what they want. It's called freedom."

"Yes..." Julie stared out the window again. "I don't really know why I'm the way I am. Perhaps it's in the genes. My mother was the ultimate housewife." She looked at Tyler again. "What about you? Where'd you get your yen for adventure?"

"Almost certainly from my dad, who was a photojournalist. I understand he loved nothing better than trekking the wilds of any country in search of any story. In fact, he met my mother in the Emergency Room of the hospital where she worked in Seattle. He'd broken his leg mountain climbing or something."

"Does it bother you to talk about him?"

"Nope."

"Good, because I'm really cur—" An earsplitting POP! drowned whatever Julie said. She screamed. More pops and backfires exploded in rapid succession. "Oh my God... oh my God..." Julie began to chant, clearly near hysteria.

Tyler, his gaze glued to the manifold pressure gauge, ignored her for the moment and assessed the situation. The inches of mercury dropped from twenty to ten before his eyes. The RPMs began to surge.

Great. Just great.

Tyler scanned the horizon for a place to land, only to remember the airstrip used by crop dusters. If he couldn't find it in the snow, he'd have to make do with one of the many fields, something he preferred not to do with a hysterical woman on board. She'd never get over the trauma, never fly with him again.

"What's the matter?" She pounded on his arm with both hands, which hurt like heck and hampered his ability to fly the plane. *"What's happening?"*

"We have a magneto problem," Tyler soothed, catching her hands, setting them firmly in her lap. "That means we're losing power. I need to land the plane. There's an airstrip around here somewhere. Look for it."

"But—"

"Look... for... it."

She obeyed at once, twisting in her seat to press her forehead and nose to the glass window on her right.

Tyler spotted the hangar, fuel pumps and a decrepit storage building near the strip before she did, but said nothing. Better to keep her occupied, he thought. Her voice, her manner revealed how frightened she was.

"There! Over there! I think I see a building and another plane on the ground. Yes, I do! That must be it."

Tyler instantly put on his earphones and flipped the radio switch, intending to broadcast an SOS before the plane dropped too far into the valley. At that moment Julie burst into tears, distracting him from the call. Torn between her distress and the need to signal for help, he hesitated, then hastily completed the SOS, including the coordinates of the airstrip. No one responded to his call.

"Hush now," he then murmured. "I'm landing the plane. We'll be on the ground in no time." Gradually Tyler began the descent. The wheels lowered with a reassuring hum. The plane glided, touched down on the snow blanketed strip with a slight bump and then rolled out until Tyler gently braked, at which time the aircraft halted completely. Tyler immediately radioed another SOS, waited a moment for a reply that did not come, then slipped off the earphones. When he killed the engine a second later, dead silence settled on them.

"Damn," Julie said with a sniff. She appeared calmer now, no doubt because they'd survived the landing, but big tears still swam in her eyes.

"You okay?" he asked softly, wishing he could've saved her this trauma.

Julie looked down at herself as if checking to be sure, then over at Tyler, to whom she gave a shaky smile. "I believe I am." She sounded surprised. "What about you?"

"Fine." He took a deep breath, not sure where to begin. What he said and did now could make or break the possibility of future flights. "Sorry about that. I checked the magnetos before we left the airport, exactly the way I always do. Everything was fine then."

"It's okay, really."

"These things just happen sometimes, Julie."

"I said it's okay."

"Odds are, every other flight will be textbook perfect."

"Tyler!"

"What?"

"I know this wasn't your fault. And I want to apologize—" she sighed "—for losing my cool. I'm not usually such a weenie. I'm just not myself today for some reason."

"You weren't *that* bad."

Julie laughed outright at the lie. "Thanks, but I know different." She shook her head, obviously embarrassed and perhaps a little bemused. "Uh, how far away is help, do you think?"

"It's a good five miles to the nearest farm. Much farther than that to an airport of any size." He hesitated, not sure how to tell her what he knew he must tell her. "There's a chance no one heard my SOS."

Her eyes narrowed. "What do you mean?"

"I got no reply to either transmission, Julie. So I don't know if the call got out before we dropped so low that the mountains blocked the signal. I'm hoping that my SOS was picked up, but their answer wasn't."

"And if that's not the case? If the SOS *wasn't* received?"

"Then no one will know what happened to us until we walk out of here for help."

"Oh God. My dad is going to be out of his mind with worry."

Tyler nodded his regret. "Yeah."

Julie glanced down at her navy blue pumps in dismay. "I'm not exactly dressed for hiking, Tyler."

"No, and neither am I, which is the reason we're going to sit right here on the off chance help is already on the way. If no one shows up by tomorrow morning, we'll dig into those boxes of mine for something warm to wear and hike right out of here."

"You mean we're going to spend the night in this plane?"

"Looks that way."

"But we'll freeze—"

"Not as long as we have a battery and gasoline. Just pretend we're camping or something. We've got plenty of food. We'll have a picnic—" He broke off, at once intrigued by her sudden smile, which had come from nowhere and now brightened the interior of the cramped cabin. "What?"

"I just remembered that we have pillows and blankets, too, plus some gorgeous quilts that looked handmade."

"They were," Tyler admitted, adding, "Are you cold already?" to discourage further questions about the quilts.

"A little," she admitted. "Probably nerves more than anything else."

Probably, Tyler agreed, but he gladly restarted the engine and turned up the heater, which soon had the cabin toasty warm again.

"You can turn it off now," she said after a minute or so. "Think you should get the blankets and maybe something to eat before it gets any darker?"

"Good idea." Tyler, who still wore his leather jacket, quickly unhooked his safety belt and slid back the seat. "We'll need to switch places so I can get out," he said, reaching out to grasp her arm and assist in the tricky maneuver. Their fit in the cabin could only be called *snug.* With a nod, Julie scooted her seat back, too, and raised her body enough for Tyler to scoot under her and into the passenger seat. She then slipped off his lap and into the other seat.

Tyler opened the door to the plane. When he climbed outside, a blast of frigid air made him catch his breath. Ducking against it, he leapt off the wing and headed to the cargo hatch. It took some unloading, several minutes of rummaging, plus a few grunts of frustration before he located the boxes he needed. But when he finally climbed back onto the wing of the plane, he clutched not only two quilts, two pillows, a blanket and warm clothes for Julie, but a sack of miniature candy bars, a bag of potato chips and a jug of apple juice.

Ducking back inside, he handed over the clothes, then playfully pulled one of the quilts over his head so she could change into them.

"Yipes!" she exclaimed a second later. "These are ice-cold."

Two seconds on that hot body of yours should fix that! Tyler thought, a sentiment he wisely kept to himself.

"There now. I'm decent."

Tyler tossed off the quilt, took a long look and grinned at his tousled-haired companion. The sweats, too large and too long, pooled at the ankles so that only the toes of his bulky wool hunting socks could be seen. The matching top, also much too big, hung nearly to her knees.

Decent? She called that *decent?*

Tyler called it sexier than hell.

Suddenly wired, he cleared his throat and thrust the bedding at her. "Wrap yourself up in the quilt."

"Okay," she said, doing as requested, then stuffing her pillow in beside her.

Tyler did the same, and once they were both settled again, spread two blankets over them. "How's that?"

"Better, but...um...does this plane have a bathroom?"

Tyler nearly choked. "Do you see one?"

"No-o-o."

"Well, what you see is what you get."

"Oh, dear."

"You can't hold it?"

"All night?"

"Okay, okay," Tyler grumbled good-naturedly. Unable to resist, he added, "But I can't believe you didn't go before we left the airport." Tossing back the blanket and his quilt, he slipped off his loafers and handed them to Julie, who stepped into them. Somehow she managed to crawl over his lap and out the door without losing the shoes, which dangled off her feet.

Before the chill of winter reached the interior of the cabin, she was back again, cheeks and fingers already pink with cold.

"That didn't take long," Tyler, back in the pilot's seat, teased, imagining what other parts of her might be pink from exposure to the elements. He reached across her to close the door.

"Shouldn't you go, too?"

Tyler grinned and shook his head. "Thanks for the reminder, Mom, but I took care of that earlier when I got this stuff."

"You rat!" she exclaimed, trouncing him with the pillow.

Loving her lighter mood, Tyler grabbed his pillow and fought back. Laughing like the idiots they surely were, both let off emotional steam for several seconds and felt better for it.

Since they'd have heat only until they ran out of gas and lights only until the battery went dead, Tyler chose to conserve both as much as possible. It wasn't as cold outside now as it would be later. The blankets served them well at the moment. As for the lights, he let the glow of a tiny light on the instrument panel illuminate their meal.

And what a meal it was. They dined royally on candy bars and chips. They sipped apple juice directly from the jug, passed back and forth. Tyler, as always at home with adventure, noted Julie's bright eyes and wide smile. Clearly she was enjoying this as much as he was. Tyler liked that.

He liked other things, too—their current rapport, her laughter, an incredible sense of rightness. It was almost as if his life had been on hold for years and was only now beginning. He felt energized, excited, expectant. He couldn't wait to find out what came next.

"Tell me about these quilts," Julie said, smoothing the one in which she'd wrapped herself.

"My grandmother made them."

"Is she still alive?"

"Yes."

"Where does she live?"

"Omaha, Nebraska."

"Is that where your mother is from, then...Nebraska?"

"What is this, *True Confessions?*"

"I just wondered." She looked hurt. "I know next to nothing about you, Tyler, and that bothers me. Can't you open up just a little?"

Tyler drew in a steadying breath. "The woman who made the quilt is my *father's* mother, not my mother's."

Julie's eyes rounded in surprise. "But I thought you never met your father."

"I never did."

"Then how...?"

"Why don't I just start at the beginning?" Tyler asked with a heartfelt sigh of surrender. She'd get it out of him one way or the other, he suspected. Might as well make it easier on both of them.

"Oh, would you?" Julie settled back and crossed her arms over her chest, as if expecting to hear an in-depth story of the life and times of Jospeh Tyler Jordan.

Tyler had to grin. Reaching out, he flipped off the light, which threw them in total darkness. In seconds, however, his eyes adjusted and the moonlit snow outside dimmed the black inside the cabin to a lighter gray.

"You know my mother and dad met in the Emergency Room at the hospital where she worked in Seattle?"

Julie nodded.

"Well, they hit it off at once. So much, in fact, that when he was released five days later, she took him home with her."

"What did her family say?"

"My mother grew up in an orphanage. There was no family to step in."

"Ah." She said it as if the word explained a lot, which it probably did. "So what happened next?"

"What do you think?" he growled. "They had an affair. She got pregnant. He flew the coop."

Julie winced. "Your poor mom."

"My mom was better off without the jerk, in my opinion, and my one childhood regret is not the fact that I never met him, but that she never found another man to take his place. Oh, she had boyfriends and all, but never for long and never anyone who could tempt her to share the rest of her life with him." For a moment he thought of his mom, an active retiree, who lived with her two cats in a condominium he'd bought for her. He should've stayed there longer at Christmas, he realized, suddenly missing the parent who'd done her level best to be both mother and father to him.

"Why, do you think?"

"Because we've always been so close, I guess."

Julie frowned at that answer right out of Tyler's thoughts. "So you think *you* were the reason she never married?"

"No, I don't think that," Tyler said, baffled by the question. Belatedly he realized she'd asked why his mother never married, not why he missed his parent.

"But you just said—"

"Yes, I did," he interjected. "I was explaining why I miss her."

"You miss your mom?" Her expression had softened.

Feeling a fool for his unwitting admission, Tyler just shrugged.

"I miss mine, too."

Her confession wrenched at his heart, and Tyler found himself blinking back sentimental tears. God, what was happening to him?

Julie sat in silence for a moment, her face sad. "It was probably a matter of trust."

"Excuse me?"

"I'll bet your mother never married because she was afraid to trust anyone else. We never forget the bad things that happen in our lives, Tyler. They haunt us forever—coloring our thoughts, impacting on our actions, even modifying our dreams. What happened to her would be enough to sour anyone on love."

"Like one plane crash soured you on all small aircraft?"

She hesitated. "Actually, I was thinking of one adventurous husband who soured me on all adventurous men."

Tyler stared at her. Did this mean she and what's-his-name weren't happily married, as Don had guessed?

"But we're not talking about me, we're talking about you. Have you never met your father even once in all these years?"

Letting her off the hook for now, Tyler reached down for the apple juice jug, uncapped it and gulped some down. "No. He died in France while on assignment when I was nine. But he'd made no attempt to contact me or my mom up until then." He started to recap the bottle, but offered it to Julie instead.

"I'll just have to go outside again if I do," she told him with a regretful shake of her head.

"So?".

"So I'm not into freezing my fanny off, thank you."

Smiling, Tyler put the juice away.

"How did you know your dad died?" Julie next asked. "Did your mother stay in touch with him?" When Tyler hesitated, she sighed. "This really isn't my business, is it?"

"No."

"But you're going to tell me, anyway, aren't you? I mean we have to talk about something. Might as well be you."

Who could deny those twinkling eyes and that hopeful smile? Certainly not Tyler Jordan, who, for some reason, found himself awash in a sea of new emotions, not the least of which was this unexplainable desire to give Julie anything she wanted and take all he could get. "Give me a kiss, and I'll tell you everything."

"Not on your life."

"But this afternoon you were willing to do a lot more than kiss me."

"That was then, this is now."

"Just one kiss, Julie. That's all I'm asking."

Julie hesitated for several seconds, then turned slightly and leaned close to brush her lips over his. Pulling back, she rested her temple on the back of the seat and just looked at him.

"You call that a kiss?" Tyler complained, though need already tested the buttons of his fly.

"I certainly do. And even if I didn't, even if I lost my head again and wanted more, I wouldn't do anything about it. It's too darn cold to fool around, Tyler."

"Might be at first," he retorted, "but not for long, honey. Not for long." When she shook her head, he gave in without further argument. "My mother did not stay in touch with my father. In fact, she'd never have known about his death if a lawyer hadn't written to us. Seems dear old Dad had a friend, to whom he'd confided everything. At my father's funeral, this friend told my grandparents they probably had another grandchild. They hired a lawyer, who hired a detective to find us."

"What happened?"

"When my mother got the letter, she called the Seevers—uh, my father's parents—who promptly flew to Seattle to visit."

"That was kind of them."

"Kind? Kind is a telephone call to say we're sorry our son destroyed your life, may we help you out now? Kind is *not* finding fault with everything from my mother's work hours, to our rented house, to my secondhand clothes, dammit."

"Oh, Tyler, they didn't?"

"Not right away, they didn't. No, they just took me home with them for a *short* visit right after Christmas so I could meet my three uncles, two aunts, various in-laws, and cousins too numerous to count."

"Weren't you scared?"

"Hell, yes, I was scared. And it had nothing to do with the fact that I'd never been away from my mother for more than a day at a time. Those people were so curious, so loud, so—" he searched for the perfect word "*—everywhere.*"

Julie laughed softly in sympathy. "Were they good to you?"

"Depends on your definition of good, I guess. They washed me, dried me, dressed me and fed me. They took me to the doctor and to the dentist. Trouble is, I didn't need washing, drying, dressing or feeding. Nor did I need the doctor or dentist. My mother might not have been as well off as they were, but she took damn good care of me from the moment I was born, and even at the age of nine, I had enough sense to recognize the insult to her good name."

"No wonder you have a problem with big, noisy families. So what'd you do?"

"I hitchhiked into town and bought a bus ticket back home with the spending money she'd given me."

"Independent little cuss, weren't you?" Julie didn't sound a bit surprised.

"You're damn right, and I'm still that way."

"I know." Now she sounded sad.

"I can't help what I am, Julie."

"Neither can I." She touched his chin, already dark with a new growth of whiskers. "We're a pair, now aren't we, Tyler? So attracted to each other, yet so stuck in our prejudices we're afraid to do anything about that attraction."

Tyler just tipped his head back against the seat and said nothing. She was right, and he knew it.

With a soft sigh Julie turned her back on him and stared out the window. Long moments passed, during which she said nothing. Tyler, listening to her even breathing, wondered if she'd fallen asleep, until she blew softly on the window and then reached out a finger to write on the frost.

JM + TJ.

Tyler caught his breath. "You hurt my feelings this afternoon."

"When?" she demanded, turning back to him.

"When you told me I'd do just fine until you found the man of your dreams."

"I'm sorry. I certainly didn't mean to hurt you. In fact, I thought you'd go for the idea, which is really the perfect arrangement for a man who isn't interested in marrying anyone. Now, of course, I've had second thoughts, and I'm glad you didn't... for whatever reason."

They stared at each other for several long moments, during which Julie wondered what was going on in that head of his. Why would a confirmed bachelor who obviously loved sex as much as he did turn down a no-strings affair? Try as she might, Julie couldn't think of a single reason.

"Did you ever see them again?"

"Who?"

"The Seevers, doofus."

"Oh, we're back to that. Yes, I saw them again. Twice a year until I graduated from high school my grandfather sent his company jet to Seattle to get me."

"That must have been a nightmare for you."

"I got used to it in time, probably because I was so fascinated by the jet." He nodded absently, his mind clearly miles and miles away.

Julie grinned and made an inspired guess. "Do we have that air time to thank for your choice of profession?"

"That air time and the most patient private pilot in the world, Brian Baker. He was one cool dude, let me tell you, and I watched him like a hawk."

"So some good, at least, came of these visits with your grandparents."

He thought for a moment. "More good than just that resulted from the contact. In fact, I learned a lot from the guys, who were all as adventuresome as my dad. They always made sure I had a physical challenge to keep me out of trouble when I visited. And while I fitted in just fine when it came to that, in other ways it was obvious that we'd never be able to bridge our cultural diversities completely."

"When's the last time you saw them?"

"Two, no, three years ago. I flew a client to Omaha. Stopped in to see my grandparents and offer a belated thank you for making me part of their family."

"You were part of their family *by birth,*" Julie gently reminded him.

Tyler laughed. "That's what they said, too."

"So you've made your peace with them?"

"More... or less."

Probably *less,* Julie thought, picking up on an undercurrent of emotion that meant there might be family issues as yet unresolved. She wasn't sure what would happen if he ever worked all the way through them, but she believed his family, and maybe even hers, would benefit, not to mention Tyler himself. He had so much love to give—love he held back in the name of freedom.

"Where'd you meet Cord?"

Julie started at the question, which exploded into her thoughts, and looked blankly at Tyler.

"Surely you didn't think we were going to talk about *me* all night."

Oh, dear... but only fair. "I met him in California when I was twenty. He was there to surf. Stayed in the same condo as me and some girlfriends."

"Love at first sight?"

"More like lust at first sight, I'm afraid. Cord had a devil-may-care charm that knocked my raging hormones for a major loop. Three days after we met we were in the sack, where we pretty much stayed until I went home." She laughed softly. "I had a heck of a time explaining why I was the only one without a sunburn, let me tell you. I never mentioned Cord, of course. Figured I'd never see him again. But six days later, there he was, standing on my front porch with a dozen roses. We were engaged in three weeks. Married in eight more."

"Marry in haste, repent at leisure?"

Julie looked sharply at Tyler. "Now what makes you say that?"

"Something you said earlier, I forget just what."

Oh, yeah. What was it about being stranded in the middle of nowhere that made a woman blab every secret? "I tried to make it work. I really did. We simply wanted different things."

"For example...?" He stared out the window at the snowscape, now tinted midnight blue. Julie looked, too, and shivered, a move that made Tyler start the engine again.

"I wanted to buy a house. He wanted to rent so that it wouldn't be hard to move if he got the urge. I wanted to have a baby. He said we should wait a year or two or three or four. I recognized right away that there was a compatibility problem, of course, but I kept thinking he'd change." Her voice trailed to silence. Her mood turned as blue as the snow outside.

As if picking up on it, Tyler reached out and took Julie's hand, lacing his fingers with hers.

"Did you love him?"

"Like crazy."

"Do you think you'd still be married to him if he hadn't been killed?" he asked.

"Since we'd been separated for three months when it happened, I guess I can safely say no." With her free hand, she touched Tyler's chin and guided his gaze to meet hers. "Don't tell anyone, okay? Dad thinks we were deliriously happy right to the end."

"Your secret's safe with me."

She gave him a smile of thanks, and centering herself in the seat again, straightened her covers by folding the edge of her quilt down over the shared blanket which was kind of scratchy. "Isn't this pattern called 'wedding ring' or something?"

"I'm clueless."

Julie traced the intersecting rings of color sewed onto the quilt. "A wise woman would settle for a quilt with wedding rings on it to keep her warm at night. Me, I prefer a flesh-and-blood man who'll slip the real thing on my third finger, left hand."

"Have your mistakes, then, taught you nothing?"

"My mistakes have taught me plenty, not the least of which is a fact my mother shared with me years ago—*Men do not change.* What you see is what you get and what you will always have. And if I'm smart, I won't tempt fate by fooling around with a Mr. Wrong I could love."

Dead silence followed Julie's speech. It stretched for one minute, then two before Tyler finally responded.

"Considering what happened between us today, I guess you're telling me I'm not a man you could love." He kept his voice flat, but Julie thought she heard an edge of pain. She eyed him in surprise...speculation...and then hope.

"Actually," she replied with a nervous laugh, "what I'm really telling you is that I've never been all that smart."

Chapter Eight

Tyler caught his breath. "What are you saying to me?"

"What are *you* saying to *me?*" Julie countered, heart suddenly hammering.

"I asked first."

And so he had. Julie searched through her muddled brain for the right answer. "I've been fascinated by you since the first moment we met eight years ago. I'd like to believe this undying attraction is nothing more than the result of incredible sexual chemistry or my lack of good sense. I'm afraid, however, there's something more there, which is why I can't let myself go when I'm with you."

"But you suggested an affair."

Julie nodded somewhat sheepishly. "I planned to hold back, stay in control of the situation."

"While we were having sex?" He sounded incredulous.

She shrugged. "Okay, so I was stupid. I quickly figured out that wasn't possible, of course, which is why my knees turned to Jell-O there in the bathroom. That hanky-panky on your bed was a very close call...for me, anyway. I know you're not in the same stew I'm in."

"You don't know squat, Julie."

"Excuse me?"

"Why do you think I was so insulted by that 'fooling around' comment?"

"I honestly haven't a clue," she admitted. "Why were you?"

"I think it's because I'm half in love with you, and it hurt to think I meant nothing more than hot sex on a cold afternoon."

Julie sat bolt upright in her seat and swiveled full around to stare at Tyler in shock. "You're lying."

"I never lie...well, not about matters of the heart. In fact, my honesty has cost me more than one girlfriend."

"And you really believe you're fifty percent in love with me?"

He nodded once, then shook his head. "Actually, fifty-five percent might be closer to the mark...there's no way of knowing until I, um, let go, too."

So she wasn't the only one holding back.

"I have to tell you something, Julie."

"I'm not sure I can stand any more good news," she murmured, eyes suddenly misty, breathing labored. Julie sank weakly back into the seat. "But go ahead."

Tyler hesitated, then cleared his throat. "Four years ago...on your twenty-first birthday...I, um...well, um..."

"What?" she prompted, turning her head to look at him. Tyler appeared extremely uneasy and wouldn't meet her gaze.

"I flew to Clear Falls intending to crash your midnight party and claim you—finally an adult—for my own."

Julie caught her breath, stunned by the confession, which was absolutely the last thing she expected to hear this night or ever.

"By chance," he continued, his voice so soft she could barely hear, "I read a local newspaper article that featured your wedding announcement—the article was over six months old. Anyway, I flew back home instead. My, um, romance with Rita began shortly after and was almost certainly a rebound affair."

"I had no idea. I never dreamed—" She broke off, at a total loss for words. "Damn, Tyler."

He gave her a sheepish grin and a shrug. "So what would you have done?"

"You mean if you had crashed my party?"

"That's exactly what I mean," Tyler said. "Would you have left with me?"

"How can I answer that? How could I possibly know?"

"Go back in time, Julie. Pretend you're at that party. Pretend you're not married. Look into your heart and tell me how you feel. I have to know. I just have to know."

"But—"

"Try it. Sit back, close your eyes and try it."

With reluctance, Julie did—settling once again into her seat, closing her eyes, reliving her twenty-first birthday party. She remembered it well, of course, since it was a triple celebration: birthday, New Year's and welcome home. By then she'd been living in Alaska with Cord and had come home for her birthday. She tried to imagine not being married, which proved impossible, so pictured Cord as he'd looked that night, dashing as always in his leather jacket and jeans. Odd, she realized, how much he favored Tyler in that getup. But was it just the clothes? Didn't he remind her of the pilot in other ways, too? His dark eyes and hair. His height and weight. His confidence, his charisma, his—

"Julie?"

—cocky smile? *Oh my gosh.* He was Tyler all over. So like him it was spooky, yet she'd never consciously acknowledged the similarities.

"Yo, Julie."

Was that, then, what had drawn her to Cord in the first place? The fact that he reminded her of Tyler? Heaven only knew, Julie realized, though she now suspected it was.

"Julie!"

Tyler's shout echoed off the cabin and woke Julie, with a start, from her trance. She found him in her face, his hands gripping her upper arms.

"What?" she shouted back at the top of her lungs, her nose only inches from his.

Tyler never blinked. "Would...you...have...left...that...party...with...me?"

"Yes," she replied. "Yes, I would if I could have! And just for the record, I think my romance with Cord was a rebound romance, too." She bit her bottom lip to stop its trembling. "I never realized it until now, and I feel...I feel *so guilty.*"

Tyler's gaze narrowed. "Why?"

"Because I married the man under false pretenses, that's why. He thought I loved him more than any other man. Hell, *I* thought I loved him more than any other man…but all the while there was someone else—" Just in time she caught herself. Her startled gaze locked with Tyler's.

"Who, Julie? Who else did you love?"

"You."

"You love me," he breathed, his grasp on her arms downright painful.

"The word is lov*ed*," Julie quickly added, "That's past tense, Tyler, and undoubtedly explains why I held my teenaged grudge against you for so long. I was in love with a fantasy."

"And how do you feel about the flesh-and-blood man you know today?"

"In all honesty, I'm not sure. Maybe I love you a little."

"Fifty percent, say?"

"I don't know."

"Fifty-five?"

"I told you *I don't know.*"

Abruptly Tyler released her. "Take off your clothes."

"What?"

"We're going to get physical. Right here. Right now." He pushed away his quilts and blankets, then slipped out of his jacket—from all appearances a man about to strip down to nothing.

Julie pulled the covers up under her chin. "You're crazy!" she blurted.

"Can you think of a better way to clear the air between us?" he asked, grabbing the hem of his sweater and pulling it over his head. "I'm holding back. You're holding back. Neither of us can help it.'' He reached for his belt. ''Don't you see where I'm going with this?''

She saw, all right. She saw herself flat on her back with Tyler on top of her—surely a miracle maneuver in that tiny cabin. Outside the plane lay snow and subfreezing weather. Yet inside they burned. It was a Technicolor fantasy that made her squirm in the seat, but did not explain Tyler's logic.

''No,'' she therefore told him, her voice a nervous croak.

He huffed his impatience. ''To figure out if we're really in love we have to let go of all our prejudices, our doubts and our fears. In other words, *we have to lose control.* Sex is the only way I know to manage that. Can you think of another?''

Julie clutched her blanket even tighter. ''We could get drunk.''

''On what? Apple juice?''

''Don't you have a bottle of whiskey stashed away somewhere?''

''I never drink and fly.''

''I thought you might keep one for medicinal purposes.''

''No. Any more bright ideas?''

Julie thought hard, but finally had to shake her head.

''Then let me help you out of my shirt.'' He reached out.

Julie slapped his hands away. ''I have no intentions of having sex with you now... or ever.''

''But this afternoon—''

''I wasn't thinking.'' She closed her eyes to the sight of his bare chest, his unbuckled belt, the buttons of his fly... all within easy reach of her twitching fingers.

"If we don't do this now, *we'll never know the truth.*"

"Exactly," Julie admitted.

"You mean you don't want to find out how we really feel about each other?"

"That's just what I mean." She sucked in a calming breath. "Would you please get dressed, Tyler? I have something to say to you, and I'll never be able to concentrate if you're half-naked."

With obvious reluctance, Tyler pulled on his sweater. When Julie handed him his jacket, he shook his head, refusing it with a terse "I'm too hot as it is."

"So am I," she admitted, tossing off her quilts. "In fact, my palms are sweating."

Tyler reached out to grasp Julie's wrist. Turning her hand over, he placed a kiss right in the damp palm, an action that made her shiver even though her temperature shot up another couple of degrees.

"You shivered just like that at my apartment earlier today, when I touched you here." He traced the curve of her breast with the back of his free hand. "You wanted me then. You want me now."

"Yes." She didn't bother to lie. The man was no fool, after all.

He shook his head in disbelief. "So the problem really *isn't* our having sex."

"I just told you it wasn't." Julie sighed. "Say we have sex. Say it does set us free. Say we find out we love each other. What then, Tyler? An affair?"

"Sounds good to me."

"Well, not to me. I want a husband. I want kids. Remember?"

"I remember."

"Can you give me those things?" she demanded, ready to end this foolishness once and for all. The man was a confirmed bachelor. There was no doubt what he would say. "Can you give up the cliffs of Acapulco for Six Flags? Can you trade in the Grim Reaper for a bunny slope? Can you, Tyler?"

He swallowed so hard she heard it. "Maybe."

"*What!*"

"Maybe." He gave her a half smile. "Don't look so shocked. People change. I've changed."

"Since when?"

"Since I started sleeping in Don's bed. Or maybe it began the moment I set foot in that house of yours. I don't know. I do know that I've begun to reassess past decisions and future goals, and I'm not so sure that I want to grow old alone."

"So buy a parakeet."

"I don't want a parakeet. I want you."

"It's a package deal, Tyler. I come complete with father, siblings, in-laws, step relatives and—"

"Responsibility."

"Exactly."

"Do you think I don't know the price of commitment?" he murmured, looking a little less sure of himself.

"I honestly doubt it."

"Well don't, because I do."

"And you still say 'maybe'?"

"Yes."

"Are you proposing to me, Tyler Jordan?"

"Not exactly."

"Then what are you saying?"

"Nothing. Everything. Who the hell knows?" He sucked in a deep breath and tried again. "All I'm trying to do is come clean without benefit of a mind-numbing sex drunk."

"Thanks, but no thanks. I don't want to know how you feel. I don't even want to know how I feel. What I want is to get on with my search for happiness—happiness you could never give me because no matter what you say, *you have not changed.*"

"And how the hell do you know that?"

"I know because your fixation with physical challenge is a result of genes handed down to you from your father. It's heredity, which cannot be altered."

"Julie, I—"

"Let me finish," she snapped, putting a hand over his mouth. "I've played second fiddle to a man's craving for adventure before. I can't tell you how many weekends I walked the floor, scared out of my mind, because my husband was addicted to danger. I *knew* that one day some deputy would come to call with news that Cord was dead. And, by God, it happened."

"He didn't die in the line of duty?"

Julie laughed bitterly. "He died looking for new places to ski on Mount McKinley. He and his buddies were too big and brave to go to a resort and ski like normal people. No, they had to ski where no man had skied before."

"I'm sorry, Julie."

"Yeah, well, so am I."

Tyler sat in silence for a moment, clearly struggling with something he wanted to say.

"Just spill it!" Julie finally prompted with a huff of exasperation.

"I...I don't want to hurt your feelings." When Julie waved away his hesitation, Tyler continued with obvious care. "Cord could just as easily have been killed by a car while crossing a street."

"But he wasn't, was he? He died looking for fun, which he put above everything else in his life. I'll never forget that, and I have no intentions of being victimized by such selfishness again."

"Selfishness? You call being true to yourself *selfish?* Maybe you should take a good look at your own life, Julie, but from *my* point of view. You're so caught up in *your* goals and *your* dreams that no one else's matter. That, ma'am, is selfishness. And I wish you the best of luck in finding someone who doesn't have a single plan of his own. God knows he'll need the free time to keep you happy."

Julie glared at Tyler, who glared right back.

Though furious enough to trounce the man, she turned her back on him instead and, stuffing her pillow next to the window, rested her head on it.

Hell—otherwise known as this plane—would freeze over before she touched Tyler Jordan again . . . even to punch his lights out.

When Tyler opened his eyes the next morning it was to find a new layer of snow on the ground and the aircraft. He glanced over at Julie, who still slept, and instantly regretted what had transpired between them the night before.

He'd insulted her, but then she'd insulted him first with her snide remark about selfishness—and that, after his painful admission to reassessing his decisions and goals. Obviously she was like every other woman he'd ever known, except, maybe, his mother. Never satisfied with just whipping men to submission, women wanted total surrender. They wanted men's souls.

Talk about selfishness.

Well, Tyler didn't intend to sacrifice his soul to Julie or any other female.

Beside him Julie stirred in her sleep and turned in the seat so that he could better see her face. Sweet heaven, but she was beautiful. Just looking at her made him want with intensity that bothered and bewildered. No other woman had ever made him feel this way. He doubted one ever would.

So what would it be like being grounded, he had to wonder. Could the thrill of rocking a baby ever match the thrill of performing acrobatics in a sapphire blue sky or diving into an emerald green ocean? Maybe if the baby were a son with Julie's topaz eyes, he thought. And then only if the boy's mamma were in his arms, too.

These thoughts puzzled Tyler until he recalled the empty ache that was all the satisfaction he got from anything he did these days. Clearly he was changing, proof that Julie didn't know everything.

Or maybe what took place was a gradual strengthening of genes contributed by his mother. Tyler owed half his psyche to her, and no one built a better nest, after all.

With a sigh of disgust at the whole issue, Tyler tossed off his quilt and stretched muscles cramped from sitting all night.

"Good morning."

He jumped and looked down at Julie, now awake and watching him.

"Morning," he said.

"Got a toothbrush on you?"

Tyler laughed. The inside of her mouth must feel as fuzzy as his. "No, but I've got some great mouthwash." He reached for the jug of apple juice at his feet. "Tastes like apple juice."

"Not until I make a quick trip outside." She sat up and glanced out the window. "No one will see me, will they?"

"Nope," Tyler said, helping her out of her tangle of quilts and blankets. Julie's borrowed clothes, too large for her, had twisted while she slept, and it took her several moments of squirming to straighten everything out. While she did that, he opened up the door, letting in morning sunshine and a gust of freezing air.

"Yipes!" Julie exclaimed even as she crawled outside. "Oh, Tyler," she called a moment later from somewhere toward the back of the plane. "It's just gorgeous out here... but don't look yet!"

He chuckled and obeyed, sitting still until she walked back to the door, when he, too, crawled outside. Julie, cheeks rosy, boarded the plane to give him privacy.

"If I were at home," she told him the moment he stepped inside again. "I'd build the biggest Frosty in the world. The snow is perfect for packing. Just perfect. Why, that ol' snowman wouldn't melt until summer."

"I was thinking of a snowball fight, myself," Tyler replied as he settled into the seat, adding, "I much prefer throwing snowballs to throwing insults."

"Oh, so do I," Julie replied. "Do you think we could just forget everything we said and did last night and go back to where we were, say, yesterday morning? If we're mad at each other when we get home, Dad will surely pick up on it, and I don't want to have to explain."

So keeping peace at home was the motive here, and not keeping peace with the pilot. Well, that was as it should be, Tyler guessed, put firmly in his place...which was really no place at all. "We can try, I guess."

"Thanks," she murmured, squeezing his shoulder. "Ready for some breakfast?"

"I think I'll settle for juice. Feel free to help yourself to last night's leftovers if you're hungry."

She did and soon nibbled on a candy bar. "What time do you want to hike out of here?"

"Actually, I've been thinking, and I've decided that you should probably just stay put."

Julie froze mid-bite. "Alone?"

Tyler nodded. "You'll be fine. More important, you'll be warm."

"But—"

"No more arguing, remember?"

"But—"

"Please?"

Julie just stared at him for a moment, then sighed. "Okay then. I'll stay here. How long do you think you'll be?"

"Considering the conditions, I'd say four to five hours at least."

"That long?"

"It won't be an easy walk."

"I don't know about this, Tyler," she murmured with a shake of her head.

"It's either that or sit here until we rot, and I've got better things to do."

"Okay. Okay. Get on with it, but please, please be careful. I'll be scared out of my mind until you get back."

Scared out of my mind. He'd heard those words before...last night when she'd talked about Cord. At once Tyler felt a pang of regret. He didn't want Julie to worry about him. She'd already worried enough for one lifetime.

Tyler gave Julie a nod, then began preparations for his walk to civilization. A quarter of an hour later found him standing outside the plane, dressed in everything warm he could find. Julie, who stood on the wing in her sock feet, looked anxious.

"For God's sake be careful."

"I always am. How about a kiss for luck?"

"Is that smart?" she asked, obviously referring to their crazy agreement to go back in time.

"Probably not, but as I recall you don't always play it smart."

"No," she admitted with a sigh. "No, I don't."

Beckoning the pilot closer, Julie threw her arms around his neck and pressed her lips to his. Tyler responded with a bear hug that took her breath, judging by her soft exhale. He didn't waste a moment of the kiss, but deepened it by delving his tongue into her mouth.

So she wanted to forget what had happened, huh?

Not while he had breath—and desire—in his body.

Deliberately he shifted his hold on her, easing one hand between their bodies so he could cup her left breast. When she didn't slug him, he followed suit with the other hand, palming both breasts through the fabric of her top until the tips grew rock hard with passion.

Or was it from the cold?

With a grunt of remembrance, Tyler ended the kiss and released Julie, who swayed on her feet and clutched the handhold. She looked a bit dazed, he thought, suddenly of half a mind to coax her back inside, rid her of those ridiculous clothes and make love to her until she understood that their passion could not be turned off and on like a radio.

But if he did that, they'd never get out of here.

So with a nod of goodbye, Tyler turned on his heel and stomped through the ankle-deep snow of the airstrip he knew would eventually take him to a narrow road that led to another road that led to a state highway that passed the beautiful farmhouse with its farmer daddy, homemaking mom, kids of all shapes and sizes and . . . a telephone.

Julie made herself a nest of blankets and quilts and settled back down in the cabin of the plane. With a glance at her watch, she noted the time—8:00 a.m.—and then closed her eyes, hoping for sleep.

It eluded her, of course.

So she sat in the cabin of the plane hugging herself and worrying as she had so many times before. A lot of things could happen to Tyler, the fearful side of her realized. He could step in a drift, vanish from view and freeze to death. He could fall and break his neck. He could get frostbite and damage his fingers and toes.

Or, a braver side argued, he could get where he was going, call for help and come back for her, all without a scratch. It wasn't *that* cold, after all, and the man was a grown-up who'd accomplished much more dangerous feats than hiking down a country road.

Sure he had...damn him. And just remembering that took Julie's mind off her foolish fears and set it on something else—namely Tyler's addiction to adventure.

Men were such idiots, she surmised with a sniff of righteous indignation. Why, if it weren't for women, there would be no homes, no families, no holiday tradition, not to mention the zillion and one other contributions that women, and women alone, made to society while men played with their toys.

And Tyler called *her* selfish.

Clearly they were nowhere near being on the same wavelength, though he certainly had the potential to be a loving, caring man capable of commitment. His mother, the nurse, had donated half his genes, after all.

But who had the patience to draw out those latent genes? Not Julie, with her biological clock set to *marriage-saving time.*

So now what?

Well, first on the To Do list was avoiding future sexual entanglements with Tyler. Second, was to kick him out of her dreams. Third was to find someone else to take his place.

At that thought Julie laughed aloud. No man alive could take Tyler Jordan's place, and if she honestly hoped one could, then she was a bigger fool than even Tyler believed.

Still...she'd try. And who knew? Maybe she'd get lucky and get herself free.

"Thanks," Tyler called out to the Simons family as he climbed behind the wheel of father Marcus's four-wheel-drive truck and shut the door. With a twist of the wrist, he set the powerful vehicle into motion and headed out the drive and down the state highway that was the first leg of his journey back to Julie.

He glanced at his wristwatch, noting the time—just after noon. He'd been gone from her four hours. A long time to sit amongst memories of tragedy, something she'd undoubtedly done. And who could blame her?

Not Tyler, who seldom worried about anyone and so didn't really know how it felt.

Did that mean he was selfish? No, Tyler decided. It meant he was smart. Selfishness was ignoring the wants and needs of others who depended on you. No one depended on Tyler, a fact he credited to good sense and careful planning. Therefore he had every right to do just what he wanted, whenever he wanted to do it.

Would Julie ever understand that?

Tyler doubted it.

So what now?

Well, first on the agenda was finding himself an apartment so he could get out of that big old house. It was a man trap, that place. And more dangerous than any cave he'd explored. Second, he'd take up a new sport, something really outrageous that would give him a sense of pride and accomplishment. Third, he'd bury himself in his work—a sure way to forget Julie.

Forget Julie? Tyler groaned. How could work make him forget her, for crying out loud? Julie was part of his work, and that wasn't good.

It took twenty minutes to reach the airstrip, thanks to poor road conditions. Julie emerged from the plane before he killed the engine of the truck and, running across the snow in her sock feet, threw herself at him the moment he stepped from the vehicle.

"You made it!" she squealed, hugging him so hard he choked and nearly stumbled.

Unrepentant, Julie wrapped her legs around his, which hampered walking. Tyler instantly boosted her up higher and, grinning, carried her back to the plane like she was some little kid.

Apparently Julie noticed the similarity, too, for when he tried to set her on the wing, she held on tightly to him and whispered, "What'd you bring me, mister?"

"I'll show you what I brought," he growled, covering her lips with his in a hungry kiss. He moved his hands over her back and hips. She did the same, adding a provocative wiggle that nearly brought him to his knees.

When they broke apart moments later, both gasped for breath. Tyler, on finally catching his, stepped close to the wing where Julie now sat, only to freeze in place when she threw up a hand to halt him.

"No," she panted.

"No?"

"No." She swallowed audibly and shook her head. "What just happened was my fault, and I apologize. It won't happen again."

So she'd been doing a little soul searching, too. "Ever?"

"Ever. While you were gone, I did some thinking—"

How had he known?

"—and I've come to the conclusion that you and I are just not right for each other."

Tyler snorted at that.

"This is serious, Tyler. As of right now, this minute, I'm never going to kiss you again."

Well, hell.

"This won't be easy."

Try *impossible.*

"But it can be done. *If* you cooperate."

Geez, Louise.

"Can I count on you?"

She didn't ask for much, did she?

"Tyler?"

"Your wish is my command, baby."

Clearly picking up on his sarcasm, Julie bristled. "Thank you. Now are we going to get out of here, or not?"

"We're outta here," Tyler told her, wishing they really were. He did not look forward to what lay ahead that day...or the rest of his life, now that he thought about it.

Chapter Nine

"I forgot to ask what Dad said when you called him," Julie told Tyler as they finally drove away from the plane about an hour later. She smoothed her skirt, which was a little the worse for being wadded up all night, and then straightened the collar of her blouse, equally wrinkled.

Tyler blanched. "Oh, hell. I forgot to."

"You forgot to?"

"I'm not used to having anyone worry about me, so it never crossed my mind. Sorry."

"That's okay," she murmured, heart sinking. The man spoke the truth. He wasn't in the habit of accounting for his whereabouts and clearly wanted to keep it that way.

The tension in the truck was thick as a brick wall and every bit as formidable a barrier, making Julie wish they'd never had their little talk—if you could call it that—back at the plane. Things would never be the same... but then, that *was* the point, wasn't it?

Neither said anything for the next couple minutes, and when the silence grew so oppressive that Julie wanted to scream, she reached out and flipped on the radio. At once the familiar refrain of a Diamond Rio song filled the truck, and she lost herself in lyrics about a man and woman who solved their problems by meeting in the middle.

Compromise. What a concept.

She gave a little. Tyler gave some, too. They worked out their differences.

And what were those differences? Julie thought for a moment, trying to put into simple words exactly what kept her and Tyler apart. She decided it was his independence of family. He honestly didn't need any kind of support group and, therefore, would never view as equal any swap of high adventure for a wife and children.

He looked on the commitment of marriage as the ultimate sacrifice—and a painful one at that. She, on the other hand, couldn't wait to assume the obligations.

Of course you can't. They're the culmination of your *lifelong dreams.*

Julie tensed at those words, which echoed so loudly in her head they might as well have been spoken. She glanced over at Tyler, who drove blissfully. Clearly he'd said nothing... at least today. Last night he'd ventilated, though, undoubtedly the reason for the errant thought.

She suddenly felt guilty for blaming Tyler because he couldn't suddenly assume her hopes and plans, abandoning, in the process, his own.

Selfish. Selfish. Selfish. The word hummed louder than the truck's big snow tires as they rolled down the asphalt.

At that moment Tyler turned off the state highway and onto a graveled drive that led to the farmhouse he'd pointed out to her from the sky yesterday. Immediately the tires sang a new tune.

Compromise. Compromise. Compromise.

Thoroughly chastised by her conscience—it had to be the culprit!—Julie shook her head to clear it and stared at the house, which was as pretty from the ground as from above. Enchanted, she climbed out of the vehicle and walked with Tyler to the door. A man and woman stepped out onto the porch to greet them, followed by five towheaded kids consisting of twin boys who looked about six or seven, a girl who looked about five and two younger boys of mystery ages.

"You poor thing!" the woman greeted Julie, reaching out to hug her even though they were strangers. "Was last night just the worst night of your life?"

"It was really kind of fun," Julie heard herself admit. Her gaze locked with Tyler's. He looked as surprised by the candid comment as she was. "I mean, we were plenty warm. We had food. I did wish I could call my dad, which I'd really love to do now if I could use your phone...?"

"Of course. Come on in."

The woman, who introduced herself as Nancy and her husband as Marcus, showed Julie to an office, then left her alone. Julie sat at a rolltop desk and picked up the telephone, but before she could dial the number, Tyler joined her.

"Just in case he wants to yell at me."

"But it wasn't your fault," she argued, listening to the phone ring. She tried the house first in hopes he was home for lunch.

"Hello?"

"Don?" What was he doing in Idaho?

"Julie! Thank God. Where are you?"

"Washington. We've had a slight...problem." Quickly Julie told everything she knew about the plane's troubles, which wasn't much. "Is Dad very upset?"

"Dad's in the hospital."

"The hospital!" Julie felt the blood drain from her face. Tyler took one good look at her, pulled out the desk chair and pushed her into it. "What happened? How is he?" All she could think of was a heart attack or stroke.

"He's okay. Well, except for the broken leg."

"Oh, my gosh! How on earth did he break his leg?"

"He wrecked his truck. When you two didn't get home like you were supposed to, he naturally got worried so decided he'd go talk to the sheriff. On the way he hit a patch of black ice and flipped the truck. His leg is broken in three different places—one above the knee, two below. Otherwise he's holding up really well... beyond worrying himself to death about you two, that is."

"Will you call him right away and tell him we're okay? Or maybe I should do it myself."

"Let me take care of it, Sis. He's taking some pain medication and is a little groggy. Then I'll call the sheriff. The law in two states is looking for you and Tyler."

"I'm so sorry. We tried to radio for help. The mountains blocked the signal or something."

"Don't worry about it. I know you would've called if you could."

"So when did you get home?"

"About an hour ago. Mrs. Brown called me last night when it happened. She had Josh. Still does."

"Josh! I'd forgotten all about him. It's a miracle he wasn't in the truck with Dad, isn't it?"

"I think so. Luckily he's got the sniffles, so Dad took him next door last night instead of dragging him to the sheriff's office. Mrs. B. said she could keep him until five."

"I'm thinking we'll be back home by then—" she glanced up at Tyler, who hovered nearby, a worried look on his face "—but I can't promise anything. We've still got to find someone to repair the plane."

"Don't worry. Kit's cutting her trip short, so between the two of us, Josharoo will be fine."

Julie and Don talked for a minute more, then she said goodbye and hung up. At once Tyler began to ask questions, which she patiently answered until he knew as much as she did, which was too darn little. Tyler shook his head in sympathy and looked for all the world like he would have loved to give her a hug, though he didn't offer it.

"I'll bet you could use a bowl of hot soup," Nancy called from the door just then. "Marcus and the kids are about to sit down with me for a late lunch. Why don't you two join us?"

"Thanks, but I'm not really hungry," Julie answered with a shake of her head. How could she eat when all she really wanted to do was fly back home and see about her dad?

"You might as well have a bowl," Tyler told her. "We're going to be here awhile."

"And you should have some, too," Nancy said, but Tyler just shook his head.

"Maybe later. Right now I've got some calls to make. We need a repairman, and we need him fast."

A good twenty minutes passed before Tyler got everything straightened out. He could hear Nancy explaining why the twins were home—water leak at school—as he joined them in the kitchen.

"Help's on the way," he reported, sitting in the chair Marcus indicated. At once the middle Simons youngster, and the only girl, got out of her chair and crawled into Tyler's lap.

He grinned and scooted back some to accommodate the child, a five-year-old named Jenny. Blond-haired, blue-eyed, Jenny had stolen Tyler's heart the first moment he met her a year and a half ago.

"Hey, princess," he said. "Are you still going to marry me?"

Jenny nodded, then solemnly pointed at Julie. "Who's she?"

"My boss," Tyler said, noting that Julie's steady gaze did not miss a thing.

"She don't love ya?"

"Nope."

"She looks like she loves ya."

Tyler grinned, now taking note of Julie's blush. "Well, she *don't,* so I'm still waiting around for you."

"Good." That said, Jenny gave him a smacking kiss on the cheek, then slipped out of his lap and returned to her chair.

"Isn't he great with kids?" Nancy murmured to Julie.

"Yes."

"I keep telling him he should settle down and have a houseful of his own."

"So do I," Julie murmured without thought, her tone dry. Tyler, suddenly the center of attention, squirmed in his chair.

Nancy bubbled with laughter. "Have you two known each other long?"

"Eight years."

"Three weeks."

Marcus looked from one to the other, obviously picking up on the tension that seemed to have followed them indoors from the truck. "Well which is it?"

"Eight years and three weeks," Tyler answered, when Julie did not.

Nancy glanced at Julie's left hand, no doubt to check for a wedding ring. When she saw there wasn't one, she got very quiet and watchful. In response to her silent speculation, Tyler took extra pains to look like a pilot whose sole mission in life was to fly the boss lady back to Idaho as soon as possible. As a result he talked a little too much, laughed a little too loud.

And when the time came to leave with the mechanic who stopped by to get them, Nancy pulled Tyler aside out on the porch.

"Before you go, you have to promise me something," she said, her voice low and full of mirth.

"What's that?"

"That you'll invite Marcus and me to the wedding."

"Whose wedding?" he asked with a frown.

"Why, yours and Julie's, of course."

Tyler's jaw dropped. "We're not getting married."

"Why ever not?"

"Because we don't love each other."

Nancy bubbled with laughter. "You men are so dense sometimes."

"I'm telling you, *we don't love each other.*"

"Tyler Jordan, I want you to look me in the eye and tell me you don't love that woman."

Tyler tried. He honestly tried. But lying—especially to friends—had always bothered him. In fact, as he'd told Julie earlier, he didn't do it at all.

Nancy laughed again. "Gotcha. So what's the problem?"

"The problem is she doesn't love me back."

Nancy sighed and pulled him into a hug that could only be called motherly. "My five-year-old daughter can see the love light shining in that woman's eyes, Ty. Don't tell me you're too blind to see it."

Love light? Get real.

"Now I want to know the real problem."

"Just call it a difference in goals."

"Meaning she wants you to settle down, and you're not so sure you're ready."

Women and their intuitions! "Maybe."

"Oh, Tyler. And to think I thought Marcus was slow." Shaking her head, Nancy stepped back. "I can see that this may take longer than it should, but when you and Julie finally get around to a wedding—and believe me, you will—I want to be invited."

Exasperated, Tyler opened his mouth to argue, then gave it up. According to Marcus, Nancy was stubborn as a burly mule. "All right. Okay. You'll be invited."

"Thanks," she said. "We'll be there with bells on."

Though Julie saw the interchange between Nancy and Tyler, she didn't ask about it until she and Tyler were once again airborne, some three hours later.

"What were you and Nancy whispering about?"

"When?" Tyler asked, never shifting his gaze from the horizon. He might as well have been in rush hour traffic and tailgating the car ahead. He concentrated that hard—or pretended to.

"On the porch. When we were leaving."

"She was telling me goodbye."

"For ten minutes?"

"Yes," he snapped. "Why?"

"Because she looked like the cat who ate the canary, that's why." Julie studied Tyler's frozen expression. The man was hiding something, and that's for sure. "You and Nancy aren't... well, you know."

"For God's sake, Julie! Of course we're not."

"Then what was she saying?"

Tyler told her about Nancy's desire to be invited to their wedding.

Julie blinked her surprise. "I assume you set her straight on our relationship."

"Of course I did."

"And did she believe you?"

"Not for a second."

Disconcerted, Julie digested that. If a total stranger could tell they were more than just co-workers or friends, how on earth would they fool her highly perceptive dad?

Tyler landed the plane at the Clear Falls airport around six that night. From there, he drove Julie straight to the hospital, where they found John in a private room, his leg elevated and iced. Don, it turned out, had already left to pick up Josh. Kit hadn't made it home yet.

"Finally!" he exclaimed, when Julie burst into the room with Tyler at her heels.

"Oh, Dad, are you okay?" she cried, throwing her arms around his neck. He looked great, she thought. Just a little tired around the eyes and perhaps a little pale.

"I'm better now that you're here, honey," he replied as he returned the hug. "What about you?"

"Just fine. We both are."

Her words drew John's gaze to Tyler, who stood back from the emotional reunion. John instantly motioned him forward, then offered his right hand to Tyler, who took, shook and released it.

"Thanks for getting her home safely," John said.

"Just doing my job," Tyler murmured, adding, "Sorry you had to worry all night. The mountains—"

"Doesn't matter now," John interjected. He looked from Julie to Tyler, then back to Julie, who saw his eyes brim with tears.

"I'm okay," she assured him, sitting on the bed to lay her head on his chest. "Really."

John swiped at a tear rolling down his face. "Your mom was right. I have no business with a plane. Why, if anything had happened to you—"

"But the airplane is wonderful!" Julie exclaimed, surprising both her dad and Tyler, from the shocked looks on their faces. "Such a timesaver. And Tyler is one heck of a pilot."

"But you went down the first time out," John said.

"Something that will probably never happen again," Julie assured him and then quoted the safety statistics Tyler had shared the day before.

When Tyler shook his head in obvious disbelief that she'd defended the plane, John began to laugh. At once his skin turned its normal shade of healthy pink, and Julie began to relax. He really was okay...except for the leg, of course.

On that thought she left the men alone, stepped out into the hall and walked to the nurses' station. A nurse there promised to find the doctor, who was supposedly on his way to the orthopedic ward at that moment, so Julie headed back to the room. Halfway there, the nurse called out to her, and, turning, Julie saw a doctor standing by the desk.

She walked quickly back.

"This is your father's physician, Kyle Lee," said the nurse.

Julie introduced herself and shook Dr. Lee's hand, then began to question him about her dad. Dr. Lee, who seemed to know his stuff, told her everything she needed to know, after which Julie walked back to the room to share the information with Tyler and her dad.

"So the doc's going to cast my leg first thing tomorrow morning?"

Julie nodded. "That's right. He said the swelling should be down enough."

"Want me to call Don with the news?" Tyler asked. He stood to Julie's left. "Better yet, why don't I go spell him? Then he and Kit can both come here and help you papa-sit tonight."

"Oh, would you?" Julie asked.

"Sure."

"Thanks a million." Rising on tiptoe, Julie brushed a kiss over Tyler's cheek. In her determination not to touch him anywhere else, she overbalanced. At once he engulfed her in a steadying embrace that pinned her to his chest.

Their gazes locked. Time stood still as memories of near intimacy washed over and warmed them. Julie caught her breath, lowered her heels and pulled free.

Cheeks flaming, she turned her attention to her dad, who watched with avid interest but said nothing.

"Well, um, later then," Tyler said, treating John to a cocky salute before he backed out the door. "Good luck."

Tyler practically ran out the door of the hospital in his haste to get some fresh air. He hopped into the company truck that had been waiting for them at the airport, a truck now loaded down with everything he owned. Tyler wished he could drive it to some apartment somewhere far away from Julie and unpack. Then and only then would he be safe from surprise passion and watchful eyes. Then and only then would he quit thinking about Julie and her claims that he was selfish.

Did a selfish man volunteer to baby-sit a hyperactive toddler? Of course not... but he might forget to phone a frantic father.

Damn, Tyler thought, more than a little irritated that he was taking Julie's accusations so seriously. Next thing he knew, he'd be second-guessing priorities that had set his whole life's course.

Irritated, borderline grumpy, Tyler parked the truck in the Newman drive and went inside the house. He explained the situation to Don, who handed him Josh and left. Not ten minutes after Don's exit—before Tyler and Josh could even get reacquainted—Kit came crashing into the house, obviously in a state of near panic over her dad. Tyler calmed her in record time and sent her back out the door, which left him and the toddler alone.

Suddenly at a loss and feeling very, very inadequate, Tyler headed to the den with the boy and turned on the television. Nothing like a little color and noise to keep a kid occupied, he thought, setting Josh on his feet on the floor in front of the big screen.

To Tyler's astonishment, the child's legs turned to rubber and would not take his weight. In addition to that, he clung to Tyler's neck much as he had Julie's one fateful Wednesday night not so long ago.

"Okay, okay," Tyler said, straightening back up with the baby hanging from his neck. "Guess TV was a bad idea. Um... are you hungry? Want some... well, hell, er, heck... I don't have a clue what you're supposed to eat." He huffed his exasperation and looked around. "Want to play cars?"

Josh shook his head—a definite no.

"How about blocks? Want to build a tower or something?"

Another negative.

"Great," Tyler muttered. "Well, what do you want to do tonight, Josh Newman?"

"Bubba," Josh told him in no uncertain terms.

Unfortunately he spoke a language Tyler had never learned... or at least did not remember. "Bubba?"

Josh nodded vigorously.

Oh, boy. Tyler looked all around the room for something—anything—that might be a bubba. "Are you wanting your brother, Tim?"

Josh gave him a blank stare, which Tyler took as a negative.

Damn. "Can you point to it?" he asked, at a total loss and highly aware of the tears now filling the toddler's huge eyes.

Josh stuck out a hand and pointed one tiny index finger to... the stairs? Game to try anything, Tyler walked to the foot of them. "These? You want to play on these?" Please say no.

Josh did say no—shaking his head so hard that his hair stood on end.

Whew. "Then you'd better point again."

Again Josh cooperated, directing Tyler up the stairs and, once they made the climb, down the hall. Certain there was a toy in Julie's room that he wanted—and oh so grateful—Tyler opened the door to that space and walked on in. He set Josh down on legs suddenly firm, then had to chase him to the bathroom where the toddler darted the moment his feet hit the floor.

"Whoa, sport!" Tyler exclaimed even as Josh ran to the tub and picked up a bottle of bubble bath with both hands.

"Bubba," Josh proudly informed him.

"Bubba," Tyler confirmed with a heartfelt sigh of relief.

Chapter Ten

Tyler's relief was short-lived. Bathing with "bubbas" turned out to be a messy, noisy, nerve-racking experience. In fact, by the time he finally coaxed a very slippery Josh from the tub almost an hour after he and his boats climbed into it, the pilot was soaking wet himself and past ready to make a crash landing on a bed somewhere.

Unfortunately Josh was not.

So the two males sat on the floor, instead, playing with the boy's noisy, red fire engine. Josh played, anyway. Tyler just watched and yawned.

Eight o'clock rolled around and then nine, but none of the Newmans returned. Exhausted and at his wit's end, Tyler scooped up Josh—fire truck and all—and carried him to Julie's bed, where the toddler usually slept. He hoped that would trigger some latent sleep reflex, and perhaps it did. At any rate, not fifteen minutes after the two of them stretched out on the bed and turned out the light, Josh abandoned the truck, snuggled close and began to suck his thumb, something Tyler had never seen him do before.

For just a second Tyler wondered if he should take the boy's thumb out of his mouth. The next moment he gave up that idea. Josh must be feeling insecure—kids sensed when all was not well—and undoubtedly needed that thumb to make him feel better. No harm could possibly come of letting Josh indulge, just for one night, in this baby habit most dentists considered bad.

Lots of habits were like that—serving a purpose at certain times, but bad if carried to excess. Drinking was one. Overeating, another. With a yawn Tyler settled back on Julie's pillow and thought of several more, counting them, instead of sheep, to get to sleep.

There was cursing, lying, speeding.

Parachuting, rafting, mountain climbing...

"I don't know about you gals, but I'm going straight to bed. Seven o'clock is going to come pretty darn early tomorrow," Don said, slipping out of his jacket and hanging it on a hook near the front door. He referred to the scheduled time of John's surgical reduction the next day. According to the doctor, the disconnected bone segments would have to be manually realigned, then casted. This required anesthesia and the help of some kind of X-ray machine, called a fluoroscope, so was considered surgery even though there was no incision of any kind.

"It sure is." Kit stifled a yawn, laughed and with a wave, headed straight up the stairs. Don followed a second later, leaving Julie alone in the den.

She sat on the couch and reached for the remote control to turn on the television, thinking to watch the late news. But in the end she didn't hear a word of it. Her thoughts focused on her dad, lying alone at the hospital. She wondered if she should've stayed there with him all night. But no, he undoubtedly slept now and wouldn't even know if she sat beside him, offering moral support.

Weird, she mused, how lonely and lost she'd felt all night, even surrounded by her family. It was almost as if someone very critical to her sense of well-being was not there.

Big brother Sid? But of course, she quickly assured herself, relieved. If Sid had been in his dad's hospital room tonight instead of overseas, she would've felt much, much better and not as if her anchor had been pulled up. He was the missing puzzle piece, not Tyler, as she'd almost feared.

Tyler.

She hoped Josh hadn't killed him. There were no blood spills on the carpet, at least. Half smiling, Julie gave up on the television and slowly trailed her siblings upstairs.

She found her bedroom dark except for a rectangle of light streaming in through the window and angling sharply up over her bed. Josh's face, cherub sweet, was just visible. The rest of his body lay shrouded in shadow. Julie noted that he sucked his thumb. Poor little guy. He must be feeling a little confused by the babysitter switch, though he seemed to like Tyler well enough.

Overcome with love for her nephew, Julie tiptoed to the bed to make sure he was covered properly. Then and only then did she realize that Josh was not alone on the bed. With a soft gasp Julie froze in her tracks. Should she just leave them alone? she wondered, the next instant deciding that might not be wise. Not only was there a chance Josh's diaper might leak—Julie doubted Tyler had thought to put the overnight kind on the boy—there was the chance Josh might roll off the bed. Julie slept lightly, always in tune to her nephew's every wiggle.

Quietly she made her way around the end of the bed to Tyler's side. She couldn't see him all that well, but could tell by his breathing—soft and low—that he slept soundly.

What a sight he was, stretched out on her bed. At once a wave of love swept over Julie, threatening to knock her to her knees.

But hadn't that happened already? Wasn't she now hopelessly lost and to a man who could not give her what she wanted?

Maybe you should want something else.

It was her conscience...once again offering unsolicited advice. Only this time Julie listened as she never had before. Maybe wanting something else *was* the answer. She wouldn't have to give up all her hopes and dreams, but just alter the ones that made living with a free spirited man impossible. They could compromise...just like in the song.

Assuming Tyler was willing.

Was he willing? Julie tried to guess but couldn't. At times he seemed so willing, almost anxious. Others, he might just as well have been in another town, state, even country. He was that distant.

Gulping back her threatening tears of frustration, Julie reached out to shake him. "Tyler?"

He did not respond.

"Tyler," she repeated, a little louder.

Tyler stirred and muttered, "Grim Reaper."

Julie, who'd understood the slurred words perfectly, bit back a sob. Some men dreamed about the women they loved. Tyler dreamed about skiing. Clearly compromise was out of the question. Her heart sank clear to her shoelaces.

"Tyler! Wake up!"

Her hissing whisper did the trick. Tyler started violently, opened his eyes and saw her, leaning over him.

"What's wrong?" he demanded, obviously confused. "What's happened?"

"Nothing. I just thought you might want to finish the night in your own bed."

"My...?" Frowning, Tyler looked over Julie's shoulder as though to find out where he was, then glanced sharply over at Josh. "Oh, yeah." With a shake of his head as though to clear it, Tyler sat up and swung his feet to the floor.

"Were you dreaming about skiing?" Julie asked as he stood.

"How'd you know?"

"You said 'Grim Reaper' right before you woke."

"Ah." Clearly a bit groggy, he moved toward the bathroom that connected their bedrooms.

"Did you win the race this time?" Julie asked, a question that brought him up short.

Tyler stood with his back to her for a second, one hand on the doorjamb, then turned half around.

"Actually I withdrew from it," he said, his expression so shadowed she could not read it. Julie could've sworn she heard a note of bemusement in his voice.

Her heart skipped a beat. Hope—ever present, ever foolish—began to burn deep inside. "Now why would you do a thing like that?"

Tyler hesitated before he spoke. "The stakes were just too damn high," he finally answered and, turning, disappeared from view.

"Mrs. Brown just called and volunteered to keep Josh all day," Don said as he poured hot coffee into an oversize mug.

"I could've done it." Tyler sat at the bar waiting for his own coffee to cool a little.

"I'd rather you came with us," Julie said. Her thoughtless comment—words she'd never have said if not preoccupied with feeding her nephew—drew everyone's gaze. "You can, um, fill in for Sid."

"Good idea..." Don said. "Unless you have other plans. I realize this isn't your problem."

"I'd be pleased to come sit with you guys," Tyler said, and Julie could tell he meant it.

After dropping Josh next door, the four of them drove to the hospital, where they talked briefly with John before searching out the waiting room. After a quick perusal of the area, Don headed to a corner and sat in one of two chairs situated on either side of a small couch. Julie sat on the couch, assuming Kit would, too. But to her surprise, it was Tyler who joined her, leaving her sister to take the other chair.

Since no one seemed to think the arrangement odd except Julie, she settled back and tried to relax. One hour and then two ticked by while Kit read magazine after magazine and Don chatted with Tyler about everything from football to fishing. Julie pretended to sleep, only half listening to their conversation until Don asked if Tyler were going to fly in the air show, come summer.

"Not this year," Tyler said—shocking words that made Julie's eyes fly open wide.

"You gonna climb Mount Everest instead?" Don questioned, obviously as surprised as his sister and twice as curious.

"Actually, I'm going to build myself a house." Dead silence followed Tyler's announcement during which Don, Kit and Julie all exchanged glances of amazement. Clearly a little on the defensive, the pilot added, "A guy's got to grow up sometime."

"Too true," Don agreed with a laugh. "And growing up isn't so bad, really. In fact, there are benefits to settling down, not the least of which is long life." He reached out and gave Tyler a playful punch. "Face it, bud, you could've broken your fool neck a thousand times in the past twenty years, and how you haven't is beyond me."

"I am one lucky guy," Tyler agreed with a solemn nod.

"So where are you going to build?" Kit asked.

"I'm not that familiar with the city yet, so I don't really know."

"You mean you're staying in Clear Falls?" Julie couldn't believe her ears.

"I thought I would." His gaze found and held hers. Something in his eyes—a message undecipherable—made Julie squirm and blush. What was with him today?

More important...what was with *her?* Wasn't it just last night she'd given up on him for good? And yet here she sat, listening to Tyler's half-formed plans and trying to find room for herself in them. Damn.

"There's the doctor," Kit suddenly announced, getting to her feet and hurrying over to the physician who'd just entered the room in search of them.

Don and Julie followed on her heels, with Tyler following more slowly, almost as if he thought he intruded or something. With a glance back, Julie reached out and grabbed Tyler's hand, pulling him closer so he could hear, too.

"Mr. Newman is doing great," Kyle Lee said. "The reduction took a little longer than I thought it would, but the bones are all in line now and the cast is in place." Dr. Lee grinned. "I think you folks are going to have your hands full with him. The cast is going to make walking next to impossible, at first, anyway, which will undoubtedly cramp his style. You might consider hiring some help, maybe even a nurse, to make him mind. Not that you couldn't handle him, Kit."

"Hey, my specialty is cancer, as you very well know. I don't do bones...especially when they belong to cranky old dads."

Dr. Lee laughed. "Then call my office. My secretary can give you the names of nurses who can handle him. Or maybe you know someone yourself."

"All right," Don said.

"How long before we can see him?" Julie asked, still holding Tyler's hand but only half-aware of it.

"He'll be back in the room in, oh—" Dr. Lee glanced at his watch "—thirty minutes, I guess. You can see him then."

"Thanks, Doc," Kit said, reaching out to shake his hand. Don did the same, and the doctor left.

The four of them walked back to their corner and sat once again.

"Do you know someone, Kit?" Julie asked.

"Not off the top of my head, but my agency surely does."

"I know a retired nurse," Tyler told them. "She worked in an ER for thirty-five years and knows her bones."

"Your mother?" asked Julie on a hunch.

"Yes," Tyler answered, grinning. "And let me tell you... Paulette Jordan is one tough cookie. Your dad might not mind her once, but I guaran-damn-tee you he won't disobey orders twice."

"Sounds like the nurse we need," Don said with a chortle. "Call her."

Tyler stayed at the hospital until he saw that John was, indeed, all right. He cherished his feeling of belonging that was a direct result of being included every time Don, Kit, Julie or even John made any kind of plans. Even all those visits with his father's relatives had not prepared him for the warmth, the kindness. Funny how he felt closer to the Newman bunch than he'd ever felt to the Seevers, but then their affection resulted from choice, not necessity.

After a meal with Don in the hospital cafeteria—the girls let them go first—Tyler headed to Mrs. Brown's and picked up Josh, who was downright glad to see him. Since the boy had eaten, he and Tyler headed upstairs where they played, napped and played some more.

Around five o'clock, Tyler went down to the kitchen and, with the help, if you could call it that, of Josh, cooked his other specialty—fried chicken. So when Don, Kit and Julie arrived home around six-thirty, they were treated to a meal that included mashed potatoes and gravy, green beans, salad and homemade biscuits.

Kit, who couldn't make toast, nearly fainted when she saw the spread.

"Look at this!" she exclaimed, seating herself at the table with enthusiasm. "You need to marry this man, Julie, and quick!"

Julie, only half in her own chair, nearly fell out of it. "Now why would you say a thing like that?" she demanded, face flushed crimson.

"Because I'm already married, doofus," Kit replied, reaching for a biscuit. "And we have to keep him in the family some way." It was only belatedly that she looked up and noticed Julie's high color. Her eyes narrowed, and she looked over at Tyler, who felt his own face grow hot. "So what's going on here?"

"Excuse me?" Julie's eyes widened in feigned innocence.

"All at once the tension in this kitchen is so thick I could cut it with this knife."

"You're imagining things," Julie said. Tyler, who could not keep his gaze off her, noticed she glued her own to her plate.

Kit sat in silence for a moment, then shrugged and began to butter the steaming biscuit she held. Tyler let out his pent-up breath in a slow hiss. All he needed was someone in the family guessing what had transpired between him and Julie. There would be hell to pay. Don, though a friend, was also Julie's big brother. Tyler did not think he'd appreciate some guy fooling around with Julie...especially if that guy wanted no more than a fling.

But was that even the case now? Or had things changed?

Looking around the table at the Newmans, now eating food he'd lovingly prepared, he knew that they had.

When, where, even how, he couldn't say, but at some point in time his priorities had changed so dramatically and thoroughly that even in his dreams he acted responsibly—like a man who knew people depended on him—and didn't mind it one damn bit.

Tyler tried this new persona on for size and found that it fit surprisingly well. In fact, he liked it. But was this just a fashion fad, here today and gone tomorrow? Or would it last as long as blue denim jeans, changing shape and style to suit the times, yet never disappearing?

After dinner everyone moved to the den, where they watched a couple of television shows. Soon bored with the sitcoms, so different from realities of his life, but reluctant to retreat to his lonely room, Tyler suggested a card game. Kit immediately picked "Spoons," a game he'd never heard of, and the five of them wound up back in the kitchen and seated around the table again.

The rules were simple: try to collect four cards of a kind, starting with a single card dealt to each player at the start of the game. To do this Tyler had to look at the cards thrust at him by Don and pass along what he couldn't use to Kit. Don, at the same time, examined cards received from Julie, who'd gotten them from Kit, who'd gotten them from Tyler. In this manner a whole deck circulated around the table several times and at lightning speed—hilarious activity that resulted in flying cards, slapped hands and howls of laughter.

The winner, if there ever was one, was supposed to reach out and get one of the three spoons lying in the middle of the table. Anyone who noticed that clandestine movement did the same, until one player—the loser!—was left without a spoon.

The game was crazy and they acted like fools—behavior no doubt resulting from a very stressful day. Josh had a ball, squealing louder than anyone and banging his own two spoons on his high chair in wild encouragement.

Finally Kit threw down her cards. "If I don't go to the bathroom right this minute I'm going to wet my pants." Belatedly and with a gasp, she obviously remembered that Tyler wasn't family. "Oh, gosh," she blurted, slapping a hand to cover her mouth. "I'm so sorry."

Tyler, pleased she considered him just another one of the bunch, had to laugh, as did Don. Julie just rolled her eyes.

Shaking her head in bemusement, Kit quickly vanished into the den.

"Well, I don't know about you guys," Don said, laying down his cards. "But I'm ready to watch the ten o'clock news and then hit the sack." He reached out for Josh. "Come on, buddy. Why don't you sleep with me tonight in 'gamp's' bed and give Aunt Julie a rest?"

"I've stolen your bed, haven't I?" Tyler murmured, just remembering.

"No sweat," Don assured him, scooping his nephew up and heading out the door.

"He sleeps around," Julie said, the next second laughing. "I mean in whatever bed is empty." She laughed again. "I mean *in this house.* Lordy, I am tired."

"So am I," Tyler said, helping her stack the cards.

She secured them with a rubber band, then tossed them in a kitchen drawer. Together they headed to the door, where she paused for a second.

"Thanks for staying with me—er, us—this morning," she said. "It meant a lot."

"To me, too," Tyler admitted. His gaze dropped to her mouth, so kissably close. It seemed like an eternity since he'd tasted her lips. Man, oh man, did he crave that sweet flavor.

"Well, good night," she murmured, easing away, crossing the den and then running lightly up the stairs.

Tyler joined Don on the couch, where they watched the news. Don then headed upstairs, too, Josh in tow, leaving Tyler alone. Exhausted, but hopelessly wide awake, Tyler watched an old movie before he finally made his way to his sleeping quarters. After undressing, he crawled into bed, turned off the lamp and lay in the dark, listening to the house grow quiet.

"Tyler?"

The word was whisper soft, but he heard it.

Or did he?

Opening his eyes, Tyler glanced at the digital alarm clock and noted the time—midnight. So he'd slept and dreamed. Maybe still did.

"Tyler, are you awake?"

No dream this, but reality in the form of Julie, who stood in the bathroom doorway and whispered his name.

"I'm awake. What's wrong?"

"Nothing," she breathed, padding across the carpet to the bed. Tyler felt the mattress dip when she sat on the edge of it, and he reached for the light.

"No, don't!" she said, laying a hand on his arm to stop him. "I didn't, um, bother with a robe."

Tyler shrugged and settled back against the pillow, waiting for her to speak again. When she didn't right away, he asked, "Are you sure nothing's wrong?"

"Positive. I just need to talk to someone about Dad." She shivered then, movement transmitted to Tyler through the mattress.

At once he touched her bare arm, covered in goose bumps.

"You're freezing," he said, tossing back the covers and patting the sheet in invitation.

Julie hesitated only a heartbeat before crawling into bed with him. Tyler covered them both again, then scooted closer.

"Put your feet on my legs," he said.

Julie obeyed, turning her back to him so that she could press the soles of her ice-cold bare feet to his warm legs. They lay like that—Julie's back to Tyler's front—for several minutes while his heat spread to and then warmed her. Tyler felt her relax against him in stages and actually wondered if she'd dozed off.

Then she spoke again. "I can't live in fear anymore."

Tyler's heart sank. So this was it. The big goodbye he'd been expecting ever since they learned of John's accident, which had surely resurrected every painful memory she'd ever had. He'd known it was coming, the reason he'd tried to hint that he could meet her halfway or even further if she was willing to try.

Obviously it wasn't going to happen. Obviously she had decided she couldn't deal with losing another someone she loved—even a someone who'd expressed a willingness to grow up. Cord had undoubtedly vowed reformation at some time or other, too, he realized. How was Julie to know that when Tyler Jordan made a promise, he kept it?

"What would you say if I told you I was going to hang up my wings forever?" he asked.

"Now why would you do that?" Julie turned over to face him. Even in the midnight shadows, he could see her astonishment.

Tyler frowned, suddenly confused. "You don't want me to?"

"Of course not. Flying is your life, your career."

So she'd chosen a farewell over requesting that he sacrifice his profession—a profession that would cause her more grief than she could bear.

"A life and career I'll gladly throw away if you'll just promise you won't say goodbye."

"Is that what you think I've come in here to tell you? Goodbye?"

"You mean... it's not?"

Julie raised herself up so that she rested her head on her left elbow and touched the fingers of her right hand to his cheek, tracing a line over the whiskers there to his lips. "I didn't come to say goodbye or even to ask you to quit flying, though you can give up the air show, if you want." She sighed. "I came to share a lesson I've learned from Dad's accident."

"And what lesson is that?" Tyler asked, capturing her fingers in his hand and then pressing her palm to his thudding heart.

"You and I made an emergency landing in the middle of nowhere, yet survived without a scratch. Dad, on the other hand, drove no more than six blocks from this house and still broke his leg."

"So?"

"So what will be, will be." She laid her head on his shoulder. "No one can predict the future, Tyler, and worrying changes nothing." She snuggled closer and kissed his cheek. "My mother once shared with me a quote of Mark Twain's. I don't remember the exact words, but the gist was that we spend most of our life worrying about things that never happen." Julie laughed softly. "Obviously she was trying to teach me a lesson. I hope she's watching from above right now so she'll know that I've finally decided to cherish every minute spent with loved ones, instead of worrying them away."

Tyler swallowed hard. "Am I one of those loved ones, Julie?"

"You are."

"And do you love me one hundred percent?"

"One hundred and fifty is more like it," she replied, her words warm against his skin.

"Good," Tyler said, rolling over so that he could look down into her eyes. He brushed her long hair back from her face, a gentle gesture that earned him her smile. "Because I love you at least that much, maybe even more." They exchanged a smile.

"I'm so sorry I badgered you about the skiing, the climbing, the jumping. You have every right to compete in any sport you want, no matter how dangerous I think it is. And I hope you win enough trophies to fill up a wall."

"I have more than enough trophies gathering dust now," Tyler said. "And not a one of them can keep me warm at night."

"I could."

"Yes. Yes, you could." Tyler hugged her hard. "Will you marry me, Julie?"

"That depends," she answered.

Tyler's heart flew up in his throat . . . until he saw the twinkle in her eye. "On what, exactly?"

"On the answer to the question I'm about to ask you."

Tyler steeled himself. "Which is . . . ?"

"Are you marrying me for my car?"

"Your . . . ? Oh, that." Damn if he hadn't forgotten all about it.

"Yes, that."

Tyler grinned. "Actually, I'm marrying you for this," he said, palming each breast. "And this." He slid his hand over her belly, then lower. His fingers dipped between her legs. "Not to mention this." His mouth covered hers in a fiery kiss. "But mostly," he continued heartstopping moments later, his voice husky with emotion. "I'm marrying you for this." Tyler embraced Julie and just held her close, stroking her hair and back, promising without words that their passion would always be grounded in solid friendship.

Julie's sigh of satisfaction told him she understood the message his body sent to hers. Her words told him just what he needed to hear. "Then yes, I'll marry you."

At once and as always, passion quickly flamed. Tyler kissed her with the hunger of years, his hands now moving urgently over her body to make up for all the time wasted since first they'd kissed and touched.

Julie moaned softly and pressed close, incredibly responsive and demanding of more. Her hands moved over his back, then dipped below the waistband of his briefs to trace the curve of his hip.

Tyler caught his breath. It was so good. So right. So perfect.

So perfect? Well, maybe not. Perfect would be a deserted island somewhere in the South Pacific, far away from man or womankind . . . not to mention children. Perfect, in other words, was another time and place.

With a groan of disappointment he threw back the covers and let in the chilly air.

"What are you doing?" Julie demanded as she was as good as kicked out of his bed.

"I just remembered where we are. Do you know who's sleeping next door, across the hall and upstairs?"

"Josh, Don and Kit?" Tyler heard the amusement in her voice.

"Exactly. And then there's your mom, looking down from above."

"Oops. Sorry, Mom," Julie murmured, waving at the ceiling, backing toward the door, where she paused, a loving smile on her face. "You'll have to get used to these thin walls if we're ever going to make all the babies I plan on making."

"Not necessarily," Tyler retorted, lying back on the pillow with his hands behind his head. His gaze feasted on every curve her satin gown clung to and revealed. "Have you forgotten I'm going to build us our own house of love?"

"I haven't forgotten, and I can hardly wait," Julie said, blowing him a kiss that was a promise of sweet, sweet things to come.

Epilogue

"Yo, Bro-in-law! Would you please drag your woman off the back porch and into this house? It's almost midnight, and we're past ready to party hearty."

Tyler grinned at Don and obediently slipped out of the room, decorated so colorfully with New Year's streamers and bobbing balloons.

Once outside, he quickly spotted his wife of eight months, standing at the far end of the porch—just where she stood the night he first fell in love with her. At once he felt a rush of wonder so intense that his eyes stung with tears.

Their marriage was a miracle of compromise for which he would always be grateful. He and Julie still had much to learn, of course, but "school" had proved so much fun that he faced every new challenge eagerly and with confidence.

"So you're not a missing person after all, but a star gazer," he gently teased.

Julie glanced her husband's way and gave him a smile that set his heart to racing. "Yes, aren't they gorgeous tonight?"

"Breathtaking," Tyler answered from the heart, his eyes on his soul mate instead of the sky.

As she had so many years ago, Julie laughed at the offhanded compliment. "Party time?"

"Yes."

"Oh." She almost sounded disappointed. Certainly reluctant.

"You don't want cake?" Tyler asked, leaning against the porch rail just to her left.

Julie shook her head.

"Well, there's also going to be ice cream. Your favorite flavor, too. Surely you want some of that."

"No, thanks."

Tyler arched an eyebrow in surprise. "What about the presents, then? There's just about a zillion of them, and you love surprises. Don't you want to open those?"

"Nope." She turned and stepped in front of Tyler, their bodies tantalizingly close, but not quite touching.

He felt her heat, saw the sexy glow in her eye, yet somehow kept his hands stuffed in his jacket pockets. "So what exactly *do* you want for your birthday?"

"You," she answered, sassy words that shimmied down his spine, warmed his heart, then finally lodged somewhere below the belt.

Emitting a to-hell-with-the-party groan, Tyler wrapped his arms around Julie and pulled her close.

"You're a wicked, wicked woman," he scolded.

"And you love me for it."

"Yeah," he whispered. "Yeah, I do."

Julie laughed, a sound of triumph and joy, then pressed her lips to his.

They kissed as they always had—honestly, hopefully, passionately. In a flash Tyler experienced the happiness and utter joy of their shared future... bright and eternal as the stars above.

* * * * *

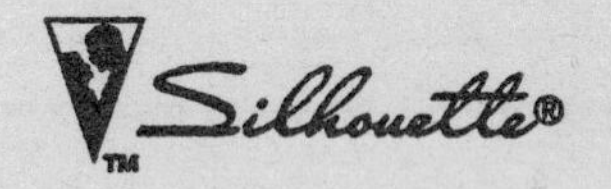
Silhouette®

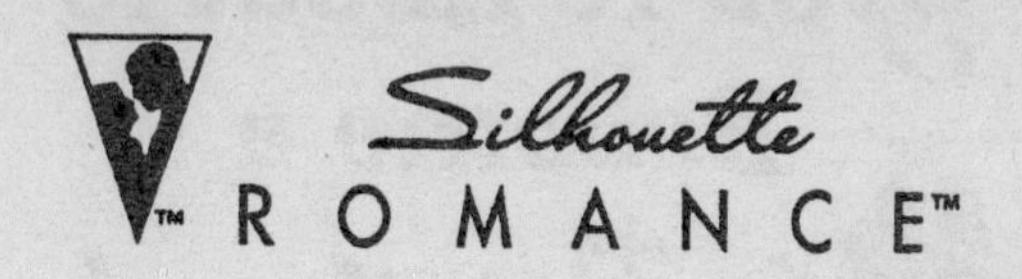

COMING NEXT MONTH

#1204 DADDY BY DECISION—Lindsay Longford
Fabulous Fathers
Charming and sexy Jonas Riley had slipped past Jessica McDonald's defenses years ago. Now the rancher was back—and proposing marriage to the single mom. But would Jonas still want Jessica when he found out the secret about her little boy?

#1205 IT'S RAINING GROOMS—Carolyn Zane
I'm Your Groom
Prudence was praying for a husband when rugged Trent Tanner literally fell from above—through her ceiling! Though Trent was no answered prayer, his request that she pose as his fiancée just might be the miracle Prudence was looking for!

#1206 TO WED AGAIN?—DeAnna Talcott
I'm Your Groom
Once Mr. and Mrs., Meredith and Rowe Worth suddenly found themselves adoptive parents to an adorable little girl. Now that they were learning to bandage boo-boos and read bedtime stories, could they also learn to fall in love and wed—again?

#1207 AN ACCIDENTAL MARRIAGE—Judith Janeway
I'm Your Groom
Best man Ryan Holt had never wanted to become a groom himself—until a last-minute cover-up left everyone thinking he was married to maid of honor Kit Kendrick! Now this confirmed bachelor was captivated by lovely Kit and wished their "marriage" was no accident!

#1208 HUSBAND NEXT DOOR—Anne Ha
I'm Your Groom
When Shelly got engaged to a nice, stable, *boring* fiancé, Aaron Carpenter suddenly realized he was in love with his beautiful neighbor, and set out to convince her that he was her perfect husband—next door!

#1209 WEDDING RINGS AND BABY THINGS—Teresa Southwick
I'm Your Groom
To avoid scandal, single mom-to-be Kelly Walker needed a husband fast, not forever. But after becoming Mrs. Mike Cameron, Kelly was soon falling for this handsome father figure, and hoping for a family for always.